Many thanks to:

Editors: Caryl Milton, Elizabeth Burns
IS Creations, Nicola Rhead, Book Cover By Design,
Brittany Urbaniak, Tracy Gray & Cariad

D1585625

REDEMPTION

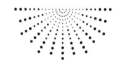

GEORGIA LE CARRE

978-1-910575-58-1

ALSO BY GEORGIA
The Billionaire Banker Series
Owned
42 Days
Besotted
Seduce Me
Love's Sacrifice
Masquerade
Pretty Wicked (novella)
Disfigured Love
Hypnotized
Crystal Jake
Sexy Beast
Wounded Beast
Beautiful Beast
Dirty Aristocrat
You Don't Own Me 1 & 2
The Bad Boy Wants Me
Blind Reader Wanted
Submitting To The Billionaire

CHAPTER ONE

RAVEN

"If only you had the courage …"

"*W*hat are you wearing to Rosa's party tonight?" Cindy asks, swinging her long shapely legs onto her manager's desk and wiggling her flawlessly manicured toes.

"I'm not going," I say, reaching for the packet of salt and vinegar crisps lying on the table.

"Why not?" she demands, her eyes flashing.

I tear the packet open. "Bed for me. I'm whacked."

She looks at me impatiently. "You're too tired to attend the hottest, biggest bash of the year?"

"It's true, I am exhausted. I didn't sleep very well last night, and anyway, what does it matter if I don't go? It's not like

Rosa and I are close. As a matter of fact, she doesn't even like me."

She stares at me. "Why do you keep saying that? It's just not true."

I shrug. "Whatever."

"I don't know where you got the impression that Rosa doesn't like you from, but you're wrong," she insists.

I pop a crisp into my mouth, crunching down with a sigh. "How come she never calls me then?"

"You know how it is with her. She's super busy."

I look at her meaningfully. "For the last five years?"

Her eyes narrow. She obviously did not realize Rosa and I have not spoken for years. "Did something happen between you guys?"

I shake my head and keep my voice casual. "Nope. When Star and I fell out, she decided to stay friends with Star and not me."

She looks at me curiously. "What happened between you and Star? The four of us were the best of friends, then one day you two were no longer on speaking terms. She won't talk about it and neither will you."

I force a smile. "Yeah, well. I guess it's all water under the bridge now."

She scrunches up her nose. "Actually, she asked about you the other night."

I feel a flash of pain in my chest. The hurt is still there. I loved Star once. "Yeah?"

"Hmmm. She asked how you were doing."

We were all in school together. The four of us. Star, Rosa, Cindy and me. We went everywhere together. We said we'd be friends forever. We even did that stupid thing of pricking our thumbs and mixing our blood. That time feels like a dream now. Unreal and faded around the edges.

How young and carefree we were. At eleven we thought the whole world was our oyster. Star wanted to be an author, Rosa wanted to be something important in the fashion industry, Cindy wanted to be a businesswoman, and I wanted to be a doctor.

Yeah, well, I was young. I was good at biology, and I didn't know what awaited me.

It all fell apart after Star found Nigel. Rosa went off to America to do her internship. I gave up my studies to help take care of my sister when she got cancer, and Cindy went on to get her university degree.

I look down at the crisps inside the packet. "Is Star coming tonight?"

"No, she's been flown away to France in her new billionaire lover's private jet," she says in a dreamy voice.

I can't help it. I pick at the scab and make the wound bleed. "So ... her marriage to Nigel is definitely ... over?"

"Dead and buried, thank god. Good riddance to that blood sucking tick." Cindy's voice has lost all its softness. It is hard with dislike.

I nod and pretend to be disinterested. "Is she ... happy?"

"Deliriously."

"That's good. I'm happy for her." True. I am happy for her. I hope she's found real happiness this time. I don't begrudge her that. I put Star out of my mind. That was all in the past. She's found her dream and I have my life to sort out.

"We seem to have gone off on a tangent here," Cindy says. "Why won't you come to the party tonight, Raven?"

"I told you, I'm tired." I stuff my mouth with a couple more crisps and chomp at them.

"Bullshit. You're letting life pass you by. Before you know it, you'll be dropping your teeth into a glass of water before bed."

"I wonder what rubbing my gums together will feel like?"

She gives me an exasperated stare. "Be serious, Raven. You have to come tonight. You'll kick yourself if you don't. It's going to be wall to wall with hot male models."

"I hate to break it to you, but most male models are gay."

"Some, Raven. *Some* of them are gay. The rest are game. David Gandy is not gay."

"David Gandy is in a long-term relationship," I say flatly.

"I know that. I wasn't suggesting you put out the red carpet for him. I was using him to illustrate the fact that there are gorgeous male models who prefer pussy to dick."

I sigh. "That's a bit of a disputable point since I don't think any gorgeous male model is going to want me when he has access to the most beautiful girls in the world."

She smiles slowly. "I bet I can make at least one male model turn and look at you."

I roll my eyes. "What're you going to do? Decorate my head with a fire cracker and sparklers?"

She shakes her head and spears me with the look that I hate. When Cindy gets that look, I watch out. She means business.

"No, but the real question is, do you accept the challenge or not?"

"No, I don't accept the challenge. You're not going to get me that way."

"As your manager, I command you to go," she says sternly.

"Look, I know you mean well and everything, Cin, but I can't go even if I wanted to."

"Why?"

"Janna," I say.

Janna is my niece. When my sister passed away three years ago, Janna's biological father didn't want anything to do with his kid, and since my mum had her hands full taking care of my disabled dad, I promised to take on the responsibility of bringing her up.

Cindy looks at me expressionlessly. "Janna is asleep at Bertha's and she will remain sleeping until the morning."

While I'm working, Janna stays with Bertha, the sweet old lady living in the apartment next door. When I get home, I use my own set of keys to slip into her spare room, pick up Janna's sleeping body and carry her back to the apartment I share with Cindy. Bertha appreciates the money and it means I can carry on earning a decent wage working as a croupier in The Diamond Rose Casino where Cindy is the manager.

"I'm supposed to tell Bertha if I want Janna to spend the whole night at her place," I remind Cindy.

"As if she will mind"

For some weird reason, an image of my sister flashes into my mind. Skeletal and hairless, she is holding my hands tightly in hers, asking me, "Do you mind very much?" Despite all the sacrifices, there has not been a moment when I have regretted my decision to bring Janna up as my own daughter.

No, Octavia, darling. I don't mind at all. I didn't mind then and I don't mind now.

Three years have passed, but thinking of her asking me that stupid question still makes my eyes fill with tears. I look down quickly and blink them away before Cindy sees them.

I clear my throat. "Bertha has been really kind and I don't want to take the piss."

"Take the piss? What are you talking about? It's not like it's going to be any trouble for her at all. Janna always sleeps right through."

I look up at Cindy. "What if she wakes up in the night and wants me?"

"Do you know how much of a little shit she is going to feel when she grows up and realizes that auntie Raven missed out on sex for years because of her? It's been so long now I bet even your vibrator tells you, you should see other people."

I roll my eyes. "My vibrator loves me. It just needs new batteries."

"What's the big plan?" she asks aggressively. "You're going to stay in every night with your vibrator until Janna becomes a woman?"

I dust the salt from my fingers. "I don't have a plan. For the moment, I'm just happy as I am."

"Girl, you can be just as happy with some dick inside you."

I sigh. "I don't have anything to wear, anyway."

"If you had would you go?"

It seems a moot question since I didn't bring any party clothes to work, and neither did Cindy. Also, it was Friday night and I still had a full shift to finish. "I might consider it," I tell her cautiously.

CHAPTER TWO

RAVEN

*A*s it happens that is a trick question. Not only has Cindy already found a replacement to cover the rest of my shift, she also has a back-up plan for my attire.

"Take your waistcoat and shirt off," she commands, standing up. Barefoot, she pads over to the door and locks it.

I don't move from my chair. "Why?"

She comes back and stands in front of me. "Just trust me, okay?"

I look at her warily.

"Please. I never ask you for anything. Just do this for me."

"You better not be making a fool of me," I warn.

Her unusually beautiful indigo eyes stare intently into mine. "Have I ever done anything to hurt you? Ever?"

"No," I admit, rising to my feet.

"Good. Now, get those clothes off."

I take my waistcoat and white shirt off while she goes to her cupboard and pulls out the waistcoat that she uses sometimes when she has to do an emergency shift. She hands it to me.

"Put it on without the shirt."

I make a face. "Why can't I just wear mine?"

"Just do it and you'll see for yourself."

I shrug into it and button up. She's a B cup and I am a full C so her waistcoat is a tight fit, and there is a lot of me on show.

"Get out of those shoes," she orders bossily, as she reaches into her bag and pulls out a pair of fake-crocodile-skin high heels.

I gasp with surprise. We saw this pair in a shop window last Sunday while we were out having lunch at the mall. I fell in love with them, but I decided not to buy them. They were pricey, and I could see no use for them in the foreseeable future. She must have gone back and got them.

"Put them on," she urges.

"They were so expensive. You shouldn't have, Cin," I protest in an awed whisper.

"Why shouldn't I have? I knew they would look terrific on you."

I bite my lower lip. I love Cindy and I don't want to insult her, but I want her to understand that I can manage on my own two feet. She doesn't need to pity me. "Because you're always paying for everything. I even have to force you to take the money for our half of the bills and now you go and buy these expensive shoes. It makes me feel as if I can't manage on my own, as if Janna and I are a charity case. If you keep doing that I'll end up feeling so bad I'll have to move out and find a different job."

She rests her butt against the edge of the desk. "Listen, Raven. I didn't tell you this before, but when my father passed away last year he left me his house in Bayswater. I could have moved there, but part of the reason I rented it out was because I didn't want to move and disrupt the arrangement we have with Bertha for taking care of Janna. There has already been too much disruption in that poor kid's life as it is, so don't you dare talk about moving out."

I sink down into the chair behind me in shock. "You did that for us?"

She shrugs. "Don't give me too much credit. I was being selfish. I enjoy living with both of you. I love little Janna and our sweet life together. So please, Raven, stop being so proud and start thinking of us as your family."

"I—"

"Do you know that Star gave Rosa and me jewelry worth more than a hundred thousand pounds? She's not doing it to show how rich she is or score points. She did it to show us that she loves us. When I give you something I can well afford I'm showing you my love."

The backs of my eyes burn.

"No tears tonight. I know you'd do the same for me if the situation was reversed." She bends down and pecks my cheek then straightens. "Talking of jewelry …"

I watch her walk to the table and dip her hand into her voluminous bag extracting a blue velvet box. "This is the only piece of jewelry you need tonight. Star gave it to me."

She takes out a choker made of white stones (since Star gave it to her I'm going to assume they are real diamonds) and red stones, again it is safe to assume they're rubies that have been designed to look like a bowtie. She dangles it in front of my dazed eyes.

"What do you say to this?"

"Wow!"

"Stand up," she orders.

Completely bemused, I obey.

She fastens it around my neck then whips away the clip holding my hair in a secure bun. It falls in a heavy curtain around my shoulders and back. She turns me around and drags me to a mirror behind the door.

"Now tell me you're not going to turn heads," she asks with a pleased expression on her face.

I stare at myself. Shocking how a diamond and ruby choker can make a simple waistcoat and black skirt look like it was purchased at some designer store. The whole ensemble actually looks hip and stylish. I touch my hair. My inky black hair is my best asset. It is long and shiny. When I was in school the boys used to call me Rapunzel.

I catch her eyes in the mirror. "It's really beautiful, but I can't wear something Star gave you. Quite frankly, I don't think she would be happy if she knew I was wearing it."

Cindy frowns. "When you give a beggar in the street a pound, do you then hang around to tell him how he must spend it?"

"No, but—"

"Star gave it to me. It is now mine and I can lend it to you, or anyone I please." She hands me a lipstick. "Slap it on," she says and moves away from me to start changing into her dress. I color my lips a deep red then turn around to watch her. Her outfit, an emerald green mini with a high neckline, is classic and luxurious. Delicately, she steps into peep-toe silver sandals and does a little twirl for me.

"How do I look?"

I smile. "Like a million dollars. When you're wearing good shoes and your hair is done properly you can get away with just about anything."

CHAPTER THREE

RAVEN

https://www.youtube.com/watch?v=HYs4Bv7jVac
Club Can't Handle Me

*T*he party is at the Elysium. We don't even need to show our purple and gold invitation card. One of the bouncers recognizes Cindy as we get out of our taxi. He lets us jump the queue that seems to snake right around the block and beyond.

Inside it is already heaving with beautiful people. We snag a couple of glasses of champagne from a passing waitress. She is dressed in something that looks like a white spacesuit. I follow Cindy as she moves deeper into the club.

"There's Rosa. Come on," Cindy shouts, and pulls me towards the roped off section marked VIP.

In the last three years I've met Rosa a few times, mostly at Cindy's birthday parties. Then she is always in jeans and fashionable though casual attire. I've never seen her in full work mode. Surrounded by glamorous women, who look as sharp as nails, she holds her own in a classic little black dress that makes her red hair almost glow under the neon lights.

When she turns and spots us she winks. In that gesture of solidarity there is warmth, confidence, and the girl I once knew. We've all grown up, but there is still that bit left over from those days when we dyed each other's hair, and slept huddled together in one tent because we scared ourselves half to death trying to outdo each other telling the most frightening ghost stories we could come up with.

Rosa excuses herself and walks over to us.

"You guys look amazing," she says as she air-kisses us. She pulls away from me. "So glad you could make it, Raven." Her eyes settle on my necklace. "Love your choker."

"It's actually Cindy's," I say awkwardly.

She smiles. "Well, it looks great on you."

"That's what I said," Cindy chimes in.

"It's a wonderful party," I say, glancing around.

"It's just warming up. Stick around and it'll get better in a while when the old school boring frats leave and the more interesting crowd is allowed in," Rosa says with a grin.

"Oh, okay."

"How's … ?"

"Janna," I supply. I know Rosa has no interest in kids. When we were younger she used to say that she was never going to have kids because she had no intention of ending up in prison for grievous bodily harm or pre-meditated murder.

"Yes, that's the one" She smiles again. "How is she?"

"Great. She's great. She's obsessed with keys."

She raises her eyebrows and nods. "She's four now, right?"

"Yup."

"That's good."

We look at each other. It's a sad moment. I realize that Rosa and I have nothing left in common.

She makes another attempt. "We must do lunch."

"Yeah, we must," I say softly.

"Let's go to that new Thai restaurant," Cindy says brightly.

Both Rosa and I turn to look at her. Neither of us had any intention of actually meeting up for lunch, but now we're stuck.

"Do you still like green curry?" Rosa asks me.

"Mmm …" I say with a smile. She remembered.

An obviously gay man with very pink cheeks and a colorful bowtie appears next to Rosa. "And who are these two charming creatures?" he asks.

Rosa introduces us smoothly and for a while we chat to him. I like him. He owns a modelling agency in Bond Street and he is wickedly funny. Eventually someone comes to claim Rosa's attention, and he moves away with her. Some people that Cindy knows come to join us. An attractive man, not really Cindy's type, asks her to dance. She wants to say no but her favorite song comes on at that very moment. She looks at me. "Wanna dance?" she asks.

"Nah, you go ahead. I'll be waiting right here," I tell her.

"You sure?"

"Go on. The song is going to be over soon."

I smile at the sight of her practically dragging the man to the floor.

A waitress passes by and I help myself to another glass of champagne. I take a sip and look around me. It's a good party but I don't belong here. A man sidles up next to me. Without turning my head I can tell he is wearing a cowboy hat.

"You're breaking my heart just standing there, sweetheart," he drawls in a strong American accent.

That amuses me. I turn towards him, and my smile dies on my lips. Oh my god!

Star is walking around the dancefloor and it is clear she is heading towards the VIP area. For a few moments I can only stare at her. She was always the beautiful one. She is even more lovely now. Her blonde hair is like a halo around her head. There is a very large man with her. Judging by the earpiece he is sporting, he must be some kind of bodyguard. Then my brain kicks in: as soon as she clears the dancefloor she will see me. My first thought is to hide. I whirl away so my back is to her, and try to think.

"Hey, do I smell or something?" the American asks.

I don't turn around. "I'm sorry, I just don't feel well," I say, and quickly start to walk in the direction of the other entrance into the VIP section. I just can't face her. Not today. I've had too much to drink and I can't deal with the past. I wouldn't even have come if I had known she was going to be here.

The man guarding the entrance lifts the rope and I walk

through. I leave my drink on a table and decide to leave the club. I'll take a taxi and send a text to Cindy when I'm home. I'll tell her I'm safe and sound. She'll be mad, of course, but I've no other choice. I hurry past the crowd of people milling about in reception and retrieve my coat.

Then I slip out into the cool night air.

CHAPTER FOUR

RAVEN

https://www.youtube.com/watch?v=YgFyi74DVjc
Written In The Stars

I walk quickly past the queue still patiently waiting to get in. There is a line of taxis looking for custom. A couple of the drivers call out to me, but I shake my head and keep on walking.

I just need to be alone for a bit. To calm myself down.

Seeing Star again after all these years hurt me. The past repeats in my mind. I see her face: accusing, tears running down her cheeks as she sobs, "I trusted you like you were my sister. How could you do that to me, Raven?"

Other memories crowd in as I walk into the night, unseeing. Lost.

I am brought back to the present with a jolt.

Three men are coming towards me. Suddenly the past disappears, my nerve endings become super sensitive, and my wits kick into gear. Oh, god, I must have turned a corner without realizing it because I am no longer on the main road, but on a deserted side street. All the business premises are closed, and there is not a soul around except me and the approaching three men.

What the hell was I thinking?

This is Elephant and Castle, not the safest place in the world to be loitering about at this time in the morning. I'm still wearing Cindy's expensive jewelry. The man in the middle is bald and bulky. He is wearing a black leather jacket and blue jeans. The other two have their hoods pulled up over their heads, making them seem sinister.

For a second I consider running back where I came from. I wouldn't get far in my new high heels if they do give chase. The temptation to cross the road is strong, but I realize that action is not going to make me any safer, in fact it may even serve to provoke them.

No, the best bet is to take my chances head on.

I swallow my apprehension, pulling my coat tighter around me so my necklace is hidden. I carry on walking forward. Instinctively, I know showing fear will only make the situation worse. As I get closer I let my gaze slide down. Not right to the ground, but low enough that there will be no eye contact.

My heart races as I get closer and closer to them.

Three feet away my gaze rises up and collides with that of the bald man. Shit. He is staring at me with an ugly expression. I instantly drop my eyes and keep on walking. My heart is thudding so hard I can hear it.

Relief pours through my veins when they walk past me.

I exhale the breath I was holding. Thank god. Thank god. It was pure paranoia, but even so. I'm still so frightened by my close call. I don't dare look back. Instead I swivel my eyes around desperately for the sight of a passing taxi. The road is completely desolate.

As I walk hastily past an alley, still debating whether I should just retrace my steps back to the club, a meaty hand suddenly reaches out from nowhere, grabs my hair, and yanks me into the alleyway.

"Gotcha," a man's voice says.

I scream with terror.

A big hand clamps down over my mouth and the other slams me against his bulk. At that moment, something strange happens. All my life I've been a non-confrontational person. I'm not ballsy like Rosa. I'm not forward like Cindy. I'd rather walk away than stand my ground. When Star accused me, I just slunk away, as if I was guilty when I was not.

But now … another part of my brain takes over. This part has 360 degree vision and misses nothing. Everything is crystal clear.

I feel the hard calluses on his palm. I smell the nicotine and taste the smoke on his fingers. He has splashed strong cologne on his neck and clothes, but underneath it, his armpits stink of stale sweat. On his breath is the reek of greasy burgers and chips. I feel the buckle of his belt dig into my back and the rough material of his jeans against my bare legs.

He is breathing hard and I know instinctively that he is one of the men who passed me by. They must have run around the block to jump me.

"Come on, come on, quick," one of the others urges. His voice is panicky.

I fumble with the catch of my purse. It opens and I slip my hand in and curl it around my mace. My purse falls to the ground. Cindy's tube of deep red lipstick rolls out, making a clattering sound on the asphalt.

I clutch my mace tightly.

The man whirls me around and throws me against a wall. A jolt of pain goes through me, but I don't let go of my mace. The wall is rough and cold. I look up at the three of them with wild eyes. Baldy is right in my face. He is twice my size. The other two have positioned themselves at either side of him.

Baldy comes right up to my face and stares at me. His eyes are dead. His hands grasp the lapels of my coat and yank it open.

"Well, well, what do we have here, little rich girl?" he taunts in an East End accent.

My thoughts are strangely calm; I need to buy myself time. I need to make them understand that I am a person just like them. I need to talk to them. Like that girl on *I Survived* who convinced her rapist not to kill her.

"I'm not rich … I have a kid, a small child," I say.

"You think I give a shit about your sob story?"

"The necklace is not mine."

"Fucking hand it over now."

"You can't have it. I told you. It's not mine to give."

His eyebrows shoot up. Violence fills his eyes. This is a man who enjoys losing his shit. Going crazy. He snarls like a wild animal. It happens so quickly I don't even see his hand move. I hear the clasp crack, and feel the burn of the necklace scraping my skin, but I am too stunned to react … until I see the necklace in his fist. Then adrenaline and sizzling fury, like I have not known before, kick in.

"I said that necklace is not mine," I scream, as I swing my hand up, my finger on the nozzle of the mace. Before I can depress the nozzle a huge, blond guy, much bigger than Baldy, suddenly appears behind the three men. He smiles at me and my eyes widen with astonishment. What the hell is going on?

With snake-like reflexes, he grabs hold of Baldy's wrist, and yanks his arm back with such force the unmistakable crack of bone breaking fills the stunned silence.

"Fuck! Motherfucker! You broke my arm," Baldy shrieks in agony as he drops to the ground.

The blond guy turns towards the hooded men. They are frozen in shock, but one of them pulls out a big knife and points it at him.

"You want to play?" Blondie asks. He is as cool as a cucumber. His accent is very slight and difficult to place. Not Russian, but Eastern Europe.

"I'll fucking cut you," Hoodie threatens. Unlike the newcomer his voice is shaking with fear and confusion. He swipes the blade through the air in a wild arc.

Blondie does nothing. Simply looks at him calmly. Hoodie lunges suddenly to stab Blondie, but he's too slow. Blondie simply side steps his attack. As Hoodie hurtles forward on his own momentum, the big, blond guy lands a lightning fast chop to his throat.

He is so unbelievably fast it's like watching something from a martial arts movie created with special effects. The hooded man collapses to his knees spluttering and gasping for breath, his face contorted into a mask of pain.

The big guy turns to face the last man. "Your turn."

He's seen what happened to his mates. He holds his palms up. "Hey man, I'm sorry," he wimps out.

"Run," Blondie tells him expressionlessly.

The second hoodie glances at his injured friends then scuttles away as fast as his legs will carry him. Blondie walks over to Baldy, who is nursing his grotesquely angled arm. Big guy puts his hand out, and Baldy, with fear in his eyes, drops my necklace into his hand.

"Go," Blondie says pleasantly.

Baldy stands with a groan of pain. He limps over to his friend who is still gasping for breath, and they move away together without a backward glance.

"You all right?" Blondie asks stretching a hand out to help me up.

My situation is embarrassing to say the least, half squatting in a dirty alleyway, but at least I haven't pissed myself yet. So there is that. I look at the offered hand, then up to his face.

The light from one of the streetlamps shines on his blond hair and part of his face. Up close he has a strong, chiseled jawline and such breathtakingly beautiful eyes they make him better looking than most of the male models at the party. Drop dead gorgeous doesn't even begin to cover him.

I look into his beautiful eyes and realize that he is far more dangerous than the men he has so effortlessly dispatched.

I raise my shaking hand and point my mace directly at him. "Don't come any closer."

Something flashes in his green eyes, then it is gone. He raises an eyebrow. "Seriously?"

"Seriously. Stay away. I don't know you."

"I just saved your ass," he says incredulously.

Slowly, I start sliding up the wall. "I can take care of myself."

His lips quirk. "Yeah it looked like that to me when I arrived," he mocks.

"I didn't need your help. I was about to mace them."

"Well thankfully, we didn't have to see how that would have worked out."

"My necklace," I say, putting my free palm out.

He drops it into my waiting palm and my hand closes over the stones. They are still warm from his skin.

"None of my business, but I wouldn't be showing something that valuable on the streets around here."

I should be thanking him profusely, but it could be the left-over fear, or the strange way I feel about him that makes me react in an uncharacteristically aggressive way. "You're right, it is none of your business."

He looks at me speculatively. "Nobody taught you manners, huh?"

With the necklace in my hand some of the fear and shock dissipate, and I realize a funny fact: I know this man. He had a beard then, but I recognize him. I've seen him in the casino. Not at my table, but playing poker two tables away. Our gazes touched once. Just once, but it was enough for me to remember him forever.

"Who are you?" I whisper.

His lips twist into an ironic smile. "Konstantin Milosevic at your service. I suppose, in this particular situation, I am ... your protector."

CHAPTER FIVE

RAVEN

I stare up at the hulking blond giant. My brain is buzzing and my heart is racing so fast my breath comes out in sharp little puffs. Those guys jumped me. That's clear. Everything after that happened so quickly my brain doesn't seem to have properly processed it yet. I need a minute to get ahold of myself again.

I take a deep breath and watch him shoot his cuffs. Slick. Calm. For a guy who just beat the hell out of three guys he is shockingly unruffled. Amazingly, even his suit has remained in impeccable condition. The practiced ease with which he took down those men now reminds me of a Hollywood action movie. I never dreamed I'd have firsthand experience of something like that in my life.

"I've seen you before," I say slowly. I'm clenching the necklace so hard the stones dig painfully into my flesh. "At the casino."

A cool smile lifts one side of his mouth. "Yes, I remember you too. You have the sexiest mouth I've ever seen on any woman."

My eyes pop open with surprise. Instead of graciously accepting the compliment and thanking him, I do what I always do and blurt out, "No, I haven't."

One dirty blond eyebrow lifts. "I must take a photograph of your mouth filled with my cock and show it to you."

My jaw hits the ground. Did he just—?

"Not now though," he says amused.

I close my mouth with an irritated snap and shake my head to clear the cobwebs floating in it. "Did you follow me here?" I ask suspiciously.

"Yes. I saw you leave the party. You looked upset, and this area is not exactly the best place for a midnight walk."

The light in the alley is too dim to see his eyes clearly, but I feel the searing heat coming from them on my skin. I stare into his eyes a moment longer. It is the only part of him that's running hot. Everything else about him feels … frozen. I glance down at the ground in confusion. Something doesn't feel right. Maybe it's not him. Maybe it's just the shock. I need to get out of this claustrophobic place.

I push off the wall. My knees are wobbling so hard I worry they'll give out and I'll be butt-kissing the ground for a second time tonight. "Thank you for your help, but I think I can manage now. You can go."

His smile melts away, leaving a detached iciness in its place. "Don't be silly. I'll walk you back to the party."

He takes a step closer and I find myself holding my breath. Alarm bells are going off in my head. Telling me to scream bloody murder. Run. Get away. This man is far, by far, more dangerous than the assholes who just tried to rob me, but I can't move.

My feet are glued to the sidewalk.

He looms over me all broad shoulders and taut, powerful limbs. I have nothing to fear from him, but even so, my heart is beating so fast I feel like a trapped bird, flapping its wings wildly. I crane my neck to look up into his face. His eyes are like magnets. Drawing me in. I can't drag my gaze away from his. My lungs feel as if they will burst. I take a shuddering breath, and the heady masculine scent of him fills my nostrils. Intoxicating me. Making it impossible for me to think.

"You are still in shock," he murmurs.

My mouth parts to speak, but my mind is a blank.

Lifting a finger, he trails it down my cheek.

The cool night air suddenly fills with sizzling electricity and an astonishing thing happens. I experience a fierce desire to lean into him, trace the curving point of his chin up past the cleanly shaven line of his jaw, wrap my legs tightly around his body, and rut with him!

The intensity and inappropriateness of the sexual urge has me bewildered.

What on earth is wrong with me? I have never wanted to do that with a complete stranger before.

I blink and try to think rationally. Maybe the attack, the horrible fear of losing Cindy's precious necklace, and this man bursting in like some modern-day hero must have shaken my bearings. That must be it.

His fingers settle on my arm, warm and firm. I want them between my legs. Oh god! This is pure madness.

I must get away from him. And quickly. Distance will help. A locked door between him and me won't hurt either. I suck in another shallow breath.

"I should get home. Now," I choke out.

"Do you need a ride?" His voice is casual.

"There is no way in hell I'm going anywhere with you." The words, raw and torn, leave my mouth without my permission. I wish I could take them back. I never meant to sound so ungrateful.

His lips purse and his icy eyes fix on me. Shit. I've pissed him off. And no wonder. The guy just rescued me and I'm acting like he's some kind of rapist leper.

"I'm sorry. I didn't mean it like that. I'm not thinking straight. It must be the shock."

He steps away from me. Getting on his haunches, he picks up my lipstick and stuffs it into my purse. I watch his fair head in a daze. He snaps it shut, stands, and holds my bag out to me. "Perhaps you will at least allow me to see you safely to a taxi." His voice is cold and disinterested.

I take my purse from him and he takes me by the elbow before I can muster a response, smartass or otherwise, and leads me out of the alley. My knees are still shaking, but the bright lights of the streetlamps help to take me out of the strange spell I was under. The world is still revolving on its axis. The waves are still rushing to the shore. Everything is still normal.

I look at him sideways as we walk back to the club.

He has money. That is perfectly clear. I've been around rich men long enough that I can tell instantly. The subtle, full-bodied richness of his cologne, the smooth tailoring of his tuxedo, the flash of the pricey cufflink at his wrist, the Swiss timepiece peeking out from the sleeve of his jacket when he dropped Cindy's necklace into my hand.

It's an unconscious habit for me to tally these things. It's useful to be able to quickly identify the high rollers, the big spenders that smile big when they win and even bigger when they lose. I've learned to recognize them as they move with easy grace from table to table because these are the men who leave the best tips.

He keeps his stride at an easy, even pace so it is comfortable for me to keep up. Our shoes hitting the sidewalk is the only sound around us.

"It's a bit of a coincidence us both being at the same party," I begin.

He spares me a lazy glance. "Not really. I'm usually at the best parties in town."

I chew my bottom lip. Something doesn't feel right. "Why don't I believe you?"

He looks amused. "Do you think I'm stalking you?"

When he says it like that it sounds utterly ridiculous. My cheeks feel as if they are on fire.

"No, I just thought … forget it."

"What's your name?"

"Why?" The sound is like the crack of a whip in the night air. I don't know why I'm being such a bitch to him. He just saved my skin and got me back Cindy's necklace. I stop walking and so does he. I turn towards him.

"Look. I'm really sorry. I don't know why I'm being so rude. I'm not usually so ungrateful and horrible. I must be in shock. Please take no notice."

There is no expression on his face.

"Maybe I just need to get out of these shoes. They're killing me."

His gaze drops down to my new shoes. They were never made for walking. A reluctant smile lifts one corner of his lips. "It does seem as if you'd have been better off just slipping your feet into the jaws of two crocodiles."

A giggle threatens to erupt from somewhere inside me. I push it back. I've embarrassed myself enough. I stretch my hand out. "I'm Raven, and it's not real crocodile skin."

He takes my hand. His is warm and firm. "Raven. It suits you." The way he purrs my name makes the hairs on my arms stand.

"My mother chose that name," I say, and instantly regret giving him that bit of useless information. As if a man like him would be interested in something like that. It is obvious that he is waaaaay out of my league. He releases my hand and I let it drop to my side.

He makes a small gesture with his right hand. "Shall we?"

I nod and we carry on walking.

A few yards ahead, the end of the queue of people waiting to get into the club comes into view. A few people turn around to look at us. I can see the women staring at him speculatively. I guess he is pretty impressive. A blond giant with extraordinary good looks.

He walks me to a taxi idling by the kerb a few feet from the entrance of the club. He opens the back door and I turn to face him. It's a nice night, mild and breezy. Strands of golden hair lift off his head and fall on his forehead. He pushes them back with his large hand. There is an air of danger and excitement around him. It's like standing very close to a wild animal, a big cat, or a grizzly bear. I feel almost dizzy with exhilaration and fascination.

"Well, this is it," he says.

I can't understand it, but an odd reluctance to part company from him fills my entire being. "Thanks for helping me. If there's anything I can do for you in return please let me know."

His eyes flash with something dark and secretive and his gaze drops to my mouth.

Heat blooms on my skin. "I mean, if there's something non-sexual," I blurt out.

His eyes widen slightly. I feel like slapping myself. What on earth has possessed me tonight? Honestly, a donkey could have managed that better. "What I meant to say is if you should one day need my help, I'll be happy to do anything I can," I say in an utterly miserable voice.

He nods gravely. "Thank you."

"Oh well. Goodnight then."

"Goodnight, Raven."

I nod and climb in. He closes the door and starts walking off in the opposite direction.

"Where to, love?" the cabbie asks, peering at me in the rearview mirror.

"Just a minute," I say, and twist in my seat to watch his progress. He strides up the sidewalk and stops in front of an outrageously expensive liquid black Lamborghini parked right outside of the club. It gleams like a black cat on wheels. A blond man in a big black machine. Yes, the car suits him to perfection.

The wing comes up and he gets in. A moment later the car races up the street, engine roaring. It hooks a tight right around the corner and disappears out of sight.

"I'm not being funny, but I need an address, sweetheart," the cab driver says with a touch of exasperation.

I whip my head around. "Sorry," I say, and give him my address.

The taxi moves and I slump back into the seat and place my hand over my belly. The truth is I feel sick to my stomach with regret. How I wish I had not been so rude to him. I should have thanked him properly.

God, I wish I could see him again. All the way home I smell his lingering scent all over me, as though he had climbed into the cab next to me.

CHAPTER SIX

KONSTANTIN

https://www.youtube.com/watch?v=XS088Opj9o0
(Frozen)

*F*uck. Fuck. Fuck. What the fuck?

I gun my car and race through the empty streets. The noise level is deafening and the buildings on either side are a blur. Dark, submerged tendrils uncurl inside my brain and begin to spin, like the eye of a fucking tornado it sucks in everything I have built. Everything that has seemed so real and so concrete comes out of the dark eye as worthless lies.

I change gears, the car screeches around the corner, and roars to a stop inside the underground carpark of my building. I leap out of the car. As I'm striding away I hit the remote the doors move downwards.

I'm so jazzed up on adrenaline. My foot taps the ground restlessly while I wait for the lift to arrive. When it opens I get into it, jab the button for my floor and step back. I can see my own reflection in the shiny surfaces of the lift doors. My hair gleams under the light and my body looks tense and tight.

The doors swoosh open at ground level, and one of my neighbors comes in. A woman. Beautiful, lush, blonde. She lives on my floor in apartment 9. The mistress of an Arab Prince. He only comes to visit during the summer months. His next trip is scheduled for the 17th of this month. She has two weeks more to wait. I know every one of my neighbors. Their habits. Their backgrounds. The likelihood of them throwing obstacles in my way.

She smiles at me. It is a friendly smile, but I've known women like her. She wants to have her cake and eat it too. She's had the money, but she's decided she needs the reassurance as well, someone to hold her and tell her how beautiful and irresistible she is. Soon, she'll be coming around to borrow a cup of sugar.

I nod distantly and stare ahead.

"You live in number five, don't you?" she asks.

I turn to look at her. "Yes."

She smiles again. "I'm in number nine."

"Right."

The elevator reaches our floor. The doors open smoothly. I raise my eyebrows to indicate that she should exit first. She gets out and waits for me.

"You should come around sometime," she offers.

"Goodnight," I say without looking at her, and go to my door.

As soon as I get into my apartment I take off my jacket and fling it onto the couch. I start removing the cufflinks from my cuffs as I walk through the vast, dimly lit hall. I leave the gold links on the dining table and begin to unbutton my shirt. I pull it out of my pants and discard it on the floor. I kick off my shoes and open the door of my training room.

I hit the lights, flick on the music, and turn it up loud.

I need to lose this tightness in my gut. I pull my undershirt over my head and chuck it in a corner. My pants join it. In the floor-length mirror on the wall opposite I can see my reflection. My muscles gleam under the spotlights.

I clench my fists. The compulsion to slam my fists against something hard is so strong it makes my biceps twinge. I indulge in this impulse often. It feels *natural* for me to turn my hands into fists. Humans might even have been genetically equipped to hit things. There is no denying that the brute solution of whacking a fist into someone's face solves a lot of problems very quickly. From day one the act of throwing a punch was not just normal but even, I realized with slight shock, a fantastic high. My whole body tingled with exhilaration.

In my boxers, I walk to the cupboard and take out a bundle of gauze ribbons. I thread the rough-woven fabric across my palms and over my knuckles. Quickly, I loop them around the webbing between my fingers and the base of my thumbs. With my hands wrapped and protected, I pull out my heavy boxing gloves from the cupboard. Slipping my hands into them I secure them, the first with my free hand and the second with my teeth. An image of her flashes into my mind. I remember the heat rising from her skin. Her smell. The way her hair trailed on my skin. Her wide frightened eyes. That damn mouth. Hell! She's a fucking innocent!

I don't need this shit.

I can't let emotion cloud my judgment.

Rolling my shoulders to release the knots of tension in them, I walk to the heavy bag hanging from the ceiling. I grab its familiar solidity with both hands, take a deep breath, and start firing off punches. I dedicate myself to a simple combination. Jab, jab, straight right; jab, straight right, left hook.

Again and again and again.

I get a good rhythm going and pound the crap out of the 100-pound bag. The whole time I keep my mind blank, concentrating only on the profoundly satisfying thumping of my gloves hitting the leather and the jarring in my bones. It feels phenomenal when my muscles are working right. It's a kind of Zen.

Upping my tempo to keep time with the music, I jog around the bag and alternate between kicking and punching it. After a few intense minutes, sweat starts running through my hair and seeping into my eyes making them burn.

I close them tight and try to focus: the bag is my enemy, but tonight the tornado in my head doesn't give me the mindless concentration I am used to. My equilibrium is fucked. I can't concentrate and it pisses me off. Control is everything to me. I control everything in my life.

Fuck it.

I want her.

I want to take her and to make her cum over and over until she is unable even to stand.

I stop suddenly, sopped in sweat, doubled over, hands on thighs, fighting to catch my breath. There's no oxygen left in my lungs. I'm unusually fatigued. I've lost my inner balance and focus. It'll be better once I fuck her, I tell myself. Once I get her out of my system, I'll be back to normal. I need to fuck her soon. Not let it become an obsession. It's just lust. Nothing more than that. Once I have her I'll be able to walk away and never look back. There has never been a woman I could not walk away from. She is just another woman. There is nothing special about her.

The music stops.

Every muscle is screaming as I walk over to the skipping rope. Soon the only sound in the room is the sound of the rope whirling, and the rapid clicks it makes when it hits the floor.

I can do this.

I am in control.

Control is me.

No woman can break down my control. None.

CHAPTER SEVEN

RAVEN

Taking off my shoes, I wiggle my toes with relief, before tiptoeing into Bertha's apartment. It is dark but I know my way through it. I quickly cross it and push open the door to the little room where Janna sleeps. Making no noise, I enter it. The room is bathed in the soft light from the small night lamp Bertha leaves plugged into the outlet at the foot of the bed.

Janna is snuggled up under a mountain of stuffed toys. One of her teddy bear's hands is covering her face. I push it away gently and look down on her. Sometimes it's painful to see how much she looks like Octavia. But, at times like this, it's good to know that a little bit of my sister is still alive in this world. As long as I can look at Janna's sweet round face, I'll see Octavia.

If things had gone differently tonight, I might not have come home at all. My hands tremble at the thought of how close I came to never seeing Janna again. How utterly reckless and foolish I was. I gather her into my arms and bury my nose in the warm crook of her neck.

As her clean, innocent scent fills my nostrils I feel my eyes well up with tears. I blink them away. Lifting her up, I carry her out of Bertha's apartment. She doesn't wake up when I put her back into her own bed and tuck her in. I kiss her forehead gently.

"I love you, baby," I whisper. "I really do and I promise I'll never take another stupid risk like that again."

"Mummy," she mumbles sleepily.

"Yes, darling," I say, but she makes an incoherent sound and goes right back to sleep. I wanted Janna to call me Aunty Raven, but the first time I took her to playschool she started calling me Mummy. It made me feel guilty to hear her calling me that, as if Octavia had never existed, never carried her in her tummy for nine months and loved her daughter with every cell in her being. It bothered me that if Octavia was watching from wherever she was she would have been sad to see that the daughter she loved so much had forgotten her. I sat Janna down and gently explained to her that I was not her mummy, Octavia was.

She looked down at the floor and mumbled, "I know that, but can't we just pretend?"

I knew then that she just wanted to be like all the rest of the children. She had not forgotten Octavia at all.

"Of course we can," I said and hugged her tightly.

Ever since then she has called me mummy. I don't know how much she remembers her mother, especially those last terrible months, but she seems happy with me. On her birthdays, we open the cards that Octavia left for her.

"How many more?" she will ask me.

Octavia left her forty cards in total so every year, I'll minus another year and tell her what is left. Then she will climb into my lap and suck her thumb as if she is still a baby. I don't tell her off for doing that. I just hold her and stroke her hair. That is my job. To hold her and love her the way Octavia would have if she was alive.

Silently, I cross the hall and continue down to my room. I set Cindy's necklace carefully on my night table. I'll have to take it to a jeweler to get the clasp fixed before I return it to her. Thankfully it looks like an easy fix. No lasting damage has been done.

I slip out of my clothes into an old, large T-shirt. Then I go to the bathroom, stand in front of the mirror and look at myself. The first thing I see are the two thin red marks on either side of my neck where the necklace burned my skin when the man ripped it off my throat. Then my gaze goes to my mouth.

My lips move. A sound comes out. "Konstantin."

An image of me kneeling in front of him sucking him off comes into my mind. His large hands are in my hair. The image is clear and so incredibly erotic, I feel a throbbing start between my legs. I shake my head to clear the picture. I don't understand why I am behaving in this way. I have never wanted a perfect stranger in this way before.

I open the mirrored cabinet, take out my make-up remover and cleanse my face. There. I feel much better now. More like myself. Normal. As I turn away from the mirror though I get a whiff of his scent. How strange. It's like I rolled around in his cologne. He barely touched me. I close my eyes and I can feel his fingers on my arm, and the heat in his eyes, as though his gaze branded me somehow.

My cellphone chirps once from my purse. I go back into my room and tug it out to look at the screen. A text from Cindy. I sent her one from the taxi to tell her I was in a cab on my way home.

Did you make it home okay?

Y es, I'm home, I type into my phone and almost instantly my phone rings.

"Why did you leave without telling me?" she asks impatiently. She must be in the Ladies, because there is no music and I can hear the sounds of women talking in the background.

"You told me Star was not coming," I accuse.

"I didn't know she was," she defends. "Anyway, you left because of that? I don't know why you're so upset with her, she was actually asking for you."

"She was?"

"Yes, she was. In fact, she said she only came because she wanted to see you again."

My knees suddenly feel weak and I lean against the dresser. "Why does she want to see me?"

"I don't know, but she wanted your number."

"Did you give it?"

"No. I thought I'd ask you first. Shall I?"

I take a deep breath. "No. Don't give it."

"Why, Raven? Whatever it is that happened between the two of you it is all in the past now. We were just kids then. She obviously wants to make up. Shouldn't you at least give her another chance? We used to be such good friends."

"I don't want to talk about it now, Cin. I'm tired and I think I'm still in shock."

"In shock? Why?"

"I almost got robbed tonight."

"What?" she screams in my ear.

I walk to my bed and curl up on it before telling her about the attack, how the three men came out of nowhere, pulled me into the alley, and broke the clasp on her necklace when they tugged it free. She listens in stunned silence, gasping every now and then.

I swallow hard, remembering the look in the bald man's eyes. "I have a feeling they didn't just want the necklace."

"Jesus, Raven."

"Then this huge blond guy comes out of nowhere. I didn't even hear him. Suddenly he appeared at the back of the men and before I knew it all three men were down."

"Was he James Bond?"

"He might as well have been. God, you should have seen him in action, Cin. It was like a martial arts movie or something. I mean, he was moving so fast, I thought I was dreaming. Afterward, he only had to straighten the jacket of his tuxedo and run a hand over his hair to smooth it back. He actually looked like he had only happened upon that unfortunate scene, and not been the one who caused it."

I use Cindy's uncharacteristic silence as an opportunity to slide under the covers, taking the scent of Konstantin with me. What if I'd let him drive me home? Would he be right here with me now, burning me alive with those hot eyes?

"Was he cute?" she asks. This is typical Cindy.

"Actually, he was hot as hell."

"Nooooo."

I laugh at her sense of drama.

"Details please!"

I give a basic rundown and keep my voice dry as if he had not affected me at all. "Tall, handsome, blond, clearly works out, exudes sex appeal at such a high level he is capable of disrupting the thought processes of any female in the vicinity." It sure disrupted mine.

"Please tell me you got his number," she says.

"I didn't," I admit, and I can't help feeling a sense of loss. Never in my life have I met such a fine man. I ruined it by being rude to him. I'll probably never see him again.

"That's a shame," Cindy says. "Never mind, the important thing is you're safe."

"Yeah, I'm safe."

"Right, I'll see you in the morning then."

"Have fun."

I bid her goodnight. The tension in my neck and shoulders has eased somewhat. Cindy has had this effect on me ever since grade school. I turn out the light. I should go to sleep. Janna's in the habit of rising well before the sun does. If I don't get some shuteye I'll be dragging serious ass tomorrow. Especially as I have an afternoon shift at the casino.

The door is locked. Janna's asleep in the next room. We're safe.

I close my eyes and picture Konstantin in the alley, standing over me, his hot eyes blazing. I have to straddle my pillow to try and stop the throbbing between my legs. I toss and turn for a long time and when I do finally fall asleep I have vivid dreams. In one I am lying naked and spread open on the floor of a dark cave. Konstantin comes in and I start sucking his cock and swallowing his cum. I wake up in the early morning hours with my panties so completely soaked I have to change them.

CHAPTER EIGHT

RAVEN

*T*he next time I wake up it is to the sound of little feet pattering down the hallway. It still surprises me at how amazing I am at this maternal stuff. Before Janna, a bomb could go off outside my window and I wouldn't hear a damned thing. Now the instant that little girl even whimpers in her sleep I'm wide-awake and streaking across the hallway.

I turn my head and there she is in the doorway, grinning from small ear to small ear, all plump rosy cheeks and crazy black curls, her favorite teddy tucked under one chubby arm. My sister in miniature. Me too, I guess. Everyone always said Octavia and I looked like twins. I smile at her slowly. What a funny monkey she is. Her top doesn't match her shorts.

"It's morning, Mummy," she sings, coming into the room with big, confident strides.

According to my alarm clock, it's just past six a.m. She actually let me sleep in today. "Is it sunny or raining?"

"It's sunny."

I lift up one corner of my duvet. "Are you going to come in for a minute?"

She slips in, her body is deliciously warm, but wriggly. I wrap my arms around her.

"Mummy?"

"Yeah."

"I've been thinking."

"Mmmm …"

"I think we should have a pony."

My eyes pop open. She looks up at me, her gaze big and innocent. Little manipulative madam.

"We could call him Harvey," she suggests sweetly.

"Forget what we could call him, where do you intend to keep him?"

"In my room of course. He can sleep with me."

"Horses don't like to live in little girls' rooms."

"Why not?" she demands.

I grin. "Because they don't like the smell of little girls' farts."

She is torn between wanting to giggle and indignation. Janna is at that age when she finds farts extremely hilarious. Her favorite story is about the chicken that farted so loudly it scared away the wolf that was going to eat it. This time though she decides that the horse is more important. "My farts are not smelly," she cries indignantly.

I put my finger on her button nose. "What about when you eat broccoli, hmmm?"

"I'll stop eating broccoli."

"No, you won't."

She wrinkles her nose. "All right I'll go out of the room when I need to fart."

"Yes, but what about when you fart while you are sleeping?"

She covers her mouth to stop herself from giggling. Then her eyes widen suddenly and she reaches out her hand to touch my neck. "What happened, Mummy?"

"I borrowed Aunty Cin's necklace last night, and I was careless when I took it off. It left a mark."

She frowns. "Does it hurt?"

"Actually, it doesn't. Are you hungry?"

"Yes. Can we have lotsa eggs for breakfast?" she asks.

"You can have whatever you like, munchkin."

"Yay! Spanish omelets with lotsa cheese and strawberry jam."

Ugh. "Yeah, sure."

She squeals with delight, hurls herself out of bed and takes off down the hallway.

"No running, kiddo! And don't wake Aunty Cindy," I shout after her, but of course, that falls on tiny deaf ears.

I haul myself out of bed. My back is more than a little sore from last night's excitement. I stretch until it pops.

Then I follow Janna to the kitchen. Just in time to see her tug open the fridge and reach for the carton of eggs on the top shelf. As it slips out of her hand, I swoop in past her, and save the eggs. Putting the carton safely on the counter next to the oven, I turn towards her.

"Sorry, Mummy. I wanted to help."

"I know, sweets, but we don't want eggs all over the floor again, do we?"

She shakes her head decisively.

"Okay, get the cheese and the rest of the ingredients out."

She runs to gather those items while I break a few eggs into a plastic mixing bowl and set it on our tiny kitchen table. She arrives with a fork. I let her beat the eggs while I grate the cheese. Then I watch her gleefully dump handfuls of cheese into the bowl.

She stirs the mixture slowly, her tiny mouth set in such a determined scowl it brings a small smile to my face.

When she is finished, I get the eggs into a pan while she sits at the table watching me.

"About my pony," she begins.

My back is to her and I smile quickly at her determination. Just like my sister she is.

I turn around. "Janna, you know we can't have a pony while we're living in an apartment, don't you?"

She sighs heavily. "Can we move to a house?"

"No, darling, we'd have to move to the country and that would be impossible right now because I have to go to work. Besides, you don't want to leave Aunty Cindy, do you?"

She shakes her head, her curls bouncing against her cheeks.

"No, I think we'd miss her too much, don't you?"

"Can we get a horse next year?"

"Maybe next year," I say, because in Janna's world next year could be tomorrow, next week, next month, or a few years from now. Any date in the future is next year to her.

Her forehead knits and she folds her arms. "Can I have a kangaroo instead?"

"Kangaroos live in Australia, sweetie. How about we get a cute little rabbit for you?"

She grins suddenly, happy again.

I serve her a plateful of eggs and she immediately spoons strawberry jam on top of it. I pour her a glass of apple juice and sit down across from her. She digs in happily. This girl loves her food and it's always a pleasure to watch her devour her meals.

"What would you like to do today?" I ask, kicking off our morning ritual.

Janna beams. "Don't you have to work today?"

"Not until this afternoon, which means, we have all morning for fun stuff."

"Yay!" she cries lifting both her hands up.

I butter a slice of toast. "So what do you want to do?"

"Can we go to the park?"

"Yes, and we can take some bread for the ducks."

She takes a bite of her toast and licks the jam from her sticky fingers. "Bertha said I was good yesterday so can I have ice cream today?"

"Oh, she did, did she?"

Janna nods fiercely, dark eyes glittering. "I was good yesterday. I was very good."

"In that case, I'll take you for ice cream."

"Yes!" she cries, clapping her little hands.

I clear the dishes while Janna finishes her juice. "If we're going to the park, what do we have to do first?"

"Clean the kitchen."

"Yes, and …," I prompt with a smile.

"Brush our teeth."

"Right! What else?"

"Get dressed real nice."

"Well, not too nice."

"Wash our faces."

"Definitely."

She leaps from the table and tears out of the kitchen, dragging her teddy bear along after her, naked feet slapping down the hallway to her room. I don't bother to tell her not to run. She's way too excited about the park. I just go after her, thinking about the park, my shift at the casino, and what Cindy has planned for us afterwards.

CHAPTER NINE

RAVEN

*T*he casino is busier than usual tonight, which is how I like it. Lots of money on the floor means plenty of action and good tips for everyone. Tonight, I'm at the blackjack table; minimum buy in is a thousand pounds.

It's not as high as some of the private tables tucked away at the far end of the casino, hidden behind curtains and velvet ropes, but I keep the cards flying and the money flows in steadily. Whenever the casino wins big (so far it has only happened once when an Arab Prince lost over five million one Tuesday afternoon) we get champagne and chocolates sent to the break room.

Six hours into my shift one of the club's regulars, a genteel South American gentleman, throws in the towel. He fishes a some chips from his jacket pocket, flips them to me, and rises from his seat. I let my lips curve into a friendly smile. The best croupiers are entertainers. You smile even when a bad loser calls you and your mother a whore. I've learned that word in so many languages I could start a dictionary. He tips his hat in an old-fashioned way and turns away and … suddenly … I'm staring Konstantin in the face.

My smile freezes as he slides into the newly vacated seat and sets down a stack of chips worth £100,000. They represent more money than I can make in two years, hefty tips included. Croupiers learn very quickly to think of them as bits of plastic. Sometimes when I used to see someone come in and lose hundreds of thousands of pounds at the roll of a die it actually hurt my soul. I couldn't help thinking, I could have bought a house with that money. In the beginning, I even used to think, for God's sake, don't place that bet. Give me the money! I won't waste it.

Konstantin hunches onto the table and stares up at me with those deep-set smoldering eyes. In the bright, glitzy lights of the casino his hair gleams like gold and his rugged good looks seem even more potent—the strong, cleanly shaven jaw, the sensual mouth lifted into a chilly smile. He's dressed beautifully in a dark suit and tie, as if he has somewhere important to go as soon as he is done here.

Did he come to this casino just to see me?

God, I hope so.

He lifts a glass of scotch to his lips. The casino is air-conditioned, but I feel hot. As if it is fire and not blood flowing in my veins. I break eye contact in the hope it'll help me regain my equilibrium, but I can feel his gaze like a scorching touch.

"Bets, gentlemen," I call, but instead of a crisp, professional invitation to play, my voice sounds cracked and scratchy.

I clear my throat and lay my hand next to the autoshuffler. There are hundreds of smoky eye cameras on the ceiling watching me as I start to pull the cards out. To my horror my butterfingers nearly drops a card. My cheeks burn as I spread the cards out on the table so the punters can see them. I sneak another glance at him, and I regret it immediately.

He is staring at me with unreadable eyes and a cold, mocking smile is playing on his lips. An image of him disarming my three assailants without batting an eye, or breaking into a sweat, flashes into my mind. Who is he, really? Why is everything so electric around him? The sizzling charge in the air makes it difficult for me to breathe. I look at those long powerful fingers, the nails impeccably manicured, and think of them resting gently on my arm. His strong pulse beating against my skin.

The thought makes me shiver, not in a bad way.

I deal the cards, but can't get my fingers to work with their usual nimble elegance. The other players don't really notice, but Konstantin keeps his dark eyes trained on my every move and I find I can barely function in the spotlight of his constant attention. To top it all the musky smell of his damned cologne keeps me off balance.

Unable to keep it together, I start making ditsy little mistakes —fumbling while dealing, dropping chips, miscounting. By the time I catch the eye of the pit boss, Konstantin is up several thousand pounds. I'm fully off my game and desperate for rescue.

Out of nowhere Cindy comes over to relieve me. She can see how frazzled I am, but there is a smooth smile on her face. I keep my gaze pointedly away from Konstantin, but I swear his body has its own gravitational pull. I have to fight the desire not to look at him.

"Are you okay?" Cindy whispers, her eyebrows drawn together as we exchange places.

"That's him," I say, barely above a murmur—the last thing I want is for him to overhear me—and her eyes widen with interest.

"Well, well," she says with a grin.

I don't hang around to find out what happens next. I just grab my shit and hurry off to finish the rest of my shift somewhere else.

An hour later, Cindy comes to find me.

"Your boyfriend was on a roll tonight."

"He's not my boyfriend," I say dryly.

"The way he was looking at you? I'm surprised your clothes didn't melt off. I know you said he was hot, but bloody hell, Raven. The guy should be an underwear model."

"He *is* gorgeous, isn't he?" I say wistfully.

"Fuck, is he? Talk about power cocks. He never stopped winning. He took us for about £150,000."

My eyes widen. "He did?"

"Yeah, he did,"

"So … he's gone?" I plaster a smile on my face even though I'm horribly disappointed. He didn't come for me after all.

"Yes, he left before I could get his number for you though."

I smile at her antics. Actually, I'm surprised she didn't get his number. Not many men can resist Cindy's charm.

"Thanks, but I kind of got the feeling if he wanted me to have his number, I'd have it by now."

"Maybe he's one of those guys who likes to play games," she speculates.

"Oh well, good luck to him, I'm done for the night. I'll see you at home?"

"See you at breakfast tomorrow."

Cindy is working the night shift so she won't be in until about seven in the morning. Usually, she makes herself a cup of tea and has breakfast with us, and if the weather is good she'll sunbathe in the garden for a couple of hours.

"I'm making pancakes," I say.

She nods. "Sounds good."

I change into my street clothes, grab my purse, and leave the staff area. There is an exit that leads right onto a back street and it is actually closer to my bus stop, but I don't take it. I used it every evening at the end of my shift—it saved me walking through the casino and lobby—but after what happened a few weeks ago, I refuse to chance it anymore. Especially, after what happened to me last night.

I go out through the front, sticking to the edge of the room. I go past the winking and bleeping slot machines, and the vast plasma screens, the deep leather sofas, and the glitzy Italian bar. I wave to the bartender, but my eyes linger on the red baize gaming tables. Cindy said Konstantin left, but what if he is still lurking somewhere close by, his lean, powerful body leaning forward, a tumbler of scotch in one hand? As I get to the lobby, I realize I was holding my breath. I let it out in a rush and shoot Bertha a text.

All well with the midget?

I step outside into the warm summer night as her answer pings.

All quiet here. The little miss lost her second tooth and went to bed at 9.

*S*till smiling at the thought of Janna's lost tooth, I glance up from my phone and come to an abrupt stop. Konstantin is at the far end of the enormous portico outside of the double entrance doors to the hotel casino. He is leaning casually against the side of his ink black Lamborghini and is obviously waiting for me!

He is dangerous to my peace of mind. I think I know that he could break my heart because there's a split second where my mind considers the cowardly option of taking off in the opposite direction, but the pulse of exhilaration tightening my chest wins out. I was hoping to find him out here.

This man intrigues me.

It's not just his looks, which are incredibly impressive, but the mystery that surrounds him, the way he disturbs the atmospheric pressure in the room. I know in my heart that he was only at that party last night because I was. He followed me outside. Why? What does a man like him want with me? I'll never know unless I get closer. And I definitely want to get closer. He's a puzzle I'm desperate to solve.

I thread through the maze of idling cars in the portico and bellhops loading suitcases onto golden luggage carts. Konstantin doesn't move, just watches me approach with those dark eyes that are going to slowly drive me insane. He straightens to his full height when I stop less than a foot away from him.

I've never felt so tongue tied in all my life as I am in this man's presence. He's most definitely stalking me—I feel an intense thrill at the thought. I just want to bury my face in the muscular curve of his neck, to breathe in that lush, virile scent, to be overwhelmed by it.

"Are you hungry?" he asks and the electricity is back, a charge running through the air that tickles the hair on my arms and infuses me with energy.

"Yes," I say.

"I know a place," he says, and steps back to pull open the door of his ridiculously expensive car. The luxurious interior of the car calls to me. I don't even weigh the pros and cons, the dangers and benefits, before I slide into it. I run my fingers over the soft leather interior as he strides around the back of the car and gets into the driver's side.

He turns to look at me with a lop-sided smile. "Ready?"

I nod and the car roars to life, the rumble shaking my bones and chattering the teeth in my head. That together with the overwhelming smell of Konstantin, the proximity of his hand as he pops the car into gear, makes my jaw clench.

"Where are we going?" I finally think to shout over the roar of the engine. Not that I care. As long as I'm home before Janna wakes up, I could quite happily speed around town with him all night.

He doesn't look away from the road, giving me an opportunity to shamelessly stare at him. The more I'm around him the more I feel it in my bones that there is something hiding in the shadows between us. Ever since I met him I've had this bizarre sensation that there's a gaping hole in my being that needs to be filled. It's primal. It's a longing. I've never experienced such a feeling before. It is as if I have walked for ages looking for this 'thing', but never even knew I was looking for it.

"Do you like Serbian food?" he asks.

"I like all kinds of food." It sounds better than admitting I've never had Serbian food, or even know any Serbian dishes.

"Excellent. We are going to a Serbian restaurant."

"Is it safe to assume you're a Serb?"

He looks over at me for a moment and I feel a tightening in my belly. The heat in the car increases exponentially and dark desires swirl around us.

"My father was," he says shortly, and turns away.

It's easier to relax when he turns his attention back to the road. I don't ask any more questions and he doesn't offer any tidbits of conversation, just keeps us moving forward, shooting us around corners, down darkened streets, buildings speeding by my window in a blur of grey. A couple of cameras flash their blue light.

"That's your third ticket," I say after the third flash. Does this guy not have to pay his traffic fines?

"Yes," he agrees pleasantly, and continues to speed us down to the East End of London. I'm not familiar with the area and I look around curiously. He brings us to a sudden stop in front of a small restaurant with Zlatibor written in faded yellow across the top. It has red awnings that are badly in need of a clean.

The car doors glide upwards, and before I can work out the least graceless way to climb out of such a low-slung car, Konstantin is already standing outside my door, his hand stretched out to me.

His fingers curl over the back of my hand, the warmth of his touch quickening my heartbeat. I feel the power in his hand as he hauls me out of the car. He holds on to my hand even when I am on my feet, and stares down at me with his signature cryptic look. I can't read him. At all. Can't even begin to imagine what's going on in that marvelous blond head of his.

He lets go of my hand and presses a button on his remote control. The car doors close, and he lightly lays a hand on the small of my back and propels me towards the entrance of the tiny restaurant.

"Don't let the shabby appearance put you off. The food is amazing," he says as we enter.

A bell jingles lightly over our heads as we enter a cramped, dimly lit dining room. It is more than half-full, but I can immediately discern that there is not a single conversation amongst the clientele being conducted in English. There is a large flat screen TV on one wall and it is playing a sports video. The colors remind me of technology from the eighties. The air is infused with the rich smell of roasting meats.

A waiter emerges through a peeling door and enthusiastically greets Konstantin in a language that I assume to be Serbian. Konstantin replies in the same language. I listen intently to the sounds they make. It sounds almost Russian. Interesting.

I didn't think this man could get more attractive, but this certainly does it. He leads us to a table in a corner. Our shoes are loud on the bare wooden floor.

We sit down at a table.

He turns to me. "Is there anything you are allergic to or won't eat?"

I shake my head and he turns back to the waiter. I watch his lips form a series of sentences I don't recognize, spellbound by the delicious smell in the air and the delicious sight of him in front of me. It's easier to enjoy him when the intensity of his attention isn't on me.

The waiter returns to the kitchen after a few more moments of indecipherable conversation. I give Konstantin a twitchy grin.

"Some women find foreign languages very sexy."

He smiles slowly. "Are you one of them?"

"I'm beginning to think I am."

The waiter reappears with two glasses of wine, sets them on the table on either side of the flickering tealight candle, and disappears again without so much as a word, Serbian or otherwise.

"I took the liberty of ordering for you," Konstantin says, lips curving into that tiny smile that tickles the hair on the back of my neck.

I should be annoyed. I don't like men who order my food for me, but I'm strangely not. In fact, I feel exhilarated. Almost high with excitement. Cindy's right, it's been too long since I've been with a man. I hadn't realized how deep that need had become—to be touched, to be kissed, to be burnt up by sizzling passion—until Konstantin brought it humming to the surface. Now that it's awake, it's demanding to be satisfied.

The dancing candlelight is playing tricks on me, his eyes seem to glow and his mouth has a cruel twist to it as he lifts his glass. "To good food eaten well."

I take a sip of the wine, relishing the taste. "What did you order?"

Konstantin shrugs, a disarming gesture that momentarily makes him seem younger. "It's a surprise, but if you truly like all kinds of food, you'll like this as well."

"Tell me about you," I invite.

He smiles and another tingling burst of electricity hisses over my skin. "What would you like to know?"

"Everything," I say, but that's ridiculous. Who asks for everything on the first date? I force a smile. "Anything."

He puts his glass of wine down and locks eyes with me. "You only need to know two things about me. I'm a businessman and I usually get what I want."

"What do you want?" My voice rasps.

"You." His eyes drop to my lips.

I laugh with a strange excitement. The sound is loud and raw. "You don't even know me."

He presses his shapely lips together, not quite smiling, his hot eyes unamused. "Then enlighten me."

"Well, you already know where I work. Stalker." I giggle, demurely this time.

He smiles this time, but tightly. Just when I think I'm peeking past the stunningly handsome facade to actually get to know him, he closes up tightly. He can't put a chill in his eyes, though. That smolder seems automatic no matter what he does with the rest of his chiseled face.

"All right." I take a deep breath. "My niece, Janna, is the most important part of my life right now."

He doesn't respond, just lifts his dirty-blond eyebrows to encourage me to continue.

I tell him about Octavia's diagnosis of stage four breast cancer and how quickly she passed away. I don't dwell on any part of it. The last thing I need is to end up in a puddle of tears.

"You're raising your sister's child on your own?" he asks, his voice incredulous, his eyes narrowed.

I shrug. "It's not quite as amazing as it sounds. She's the sweetest most adorable little tornado and taking care of her is really fun." I crinkle my nose. "Actually, I love her so much I can't even imagine my life without her now."

He stares at me.

The waiter returns from the kitchen, two large trays balanced on his palms. He sets the steaming platters of grilled meat on the table. Delicious aromas fill my nostrils as I stare at the food. He gives each of us an empty dinner plate before exchanging a few words with Konstantin and receding into the kitchen again.

He points to the different types of meat, tells me their names and describes them. There is minced beef enveloped in vine leaves, pickled cabbage stuffed with pork and rice. Serbian beans, roast meat in pastry leaves, lamb baked with eggs and potatoes. Meat patties made from veal and grilled with onions.

As he finishes explaining, side dishes arrive and I laugh. There is absolutely no way two people are going to be able to eat all this food.

"Bon appétit," he says and we begin to eat.

The meat is cooked to perfection and melts on my tongue.

"Good?" he asks.

I nod. Between luscious bites of seasoned meat and grilled veggies I carry on telling him about Janna. It's a safe topic and easy for me to talk about. Besides, focusing on the munchkin relieves some of the tension building between us. I can still barely look him in the eye.

Often I catch myself staring at his seductive mouth while trying to avoid imagining it tracing a hot line down the side of my neck. He eats slowly, taking small bites and watching me intently as he chews, his light eyes never wavering. I've never had anyone pay such close attention to me and what I was saying before.

It works on me like a drug, making me woozy, or maybe that's the wine. The waiter brought out another bottle while I was chattering on and Konstantin keeps refilling my glass while neglecting his own. I only realize after we've finished our meal that he now knows way too much about me, but the only things I know about him is he's a businessman who always gets what he wants.

The waiter arrives with a bottle of alcohol.

I start shaking my head. "I'd better not have anything else to drink." My cheeks feel flushed and warm.

"You can't say no to plum brandy," he cajoles.

Plum brandy. "Well, okay then, maybe just one glass." The waiter pours a generous measure into our glasses.

"Come. We will take our brandy out onto the patio?"

He stands and helps me out of my seat. My legs are wobbly, but I make it without incident through a dimly lit corridor to the rear of the restaurant, and out onto a patio overlooking a small private garden. There are a few tables with lanterns on them.

"They grow their own herbs and vegetables here," he tells me, and I realize how close he is. Just an inch away, a centimeter, the distance closing fast.

I turn my eyes to the sight of the rows of plants, afraid to face him afraid of what will happen if I look into his eyes and let any of the raw heat of his appeal get to me. I stare unseeing at the raised beds. That well of need within me deepens. I haven't kissed a man since Octavia got sick. That's more than two years ago.

He touches the side of my neck with a single finger. It obliterates any lingering hesitation. I can't stop myself, can't close up again. I turn to face him, lifting my chin, my lips parted. He drops his head to close the distance between us. His arms close around me, pressing me into him. I can feel the glasses of brandy cold and smooth against my back. God. I'm so wet for him. My body opens to him like a needy flower. I've waited so damn long ... and he's just what I need right now.

Then his lips lock onto mine.

His tongue slides into my mouth. Nothing is sweeter than the taste of wine on his tongue, our warm bodies struggling against each other, trying to get even closer. I want as much of this heat as I can get. That simmering smolder doesn't just live in his eyes. I can feel it humming beneath his skin, running up the front of his body.

I rise up onto my tiptoes, wrap my arms around his neck and kiss him instead of thinking, instead of breathing. He grabs my hips and angles me into the hard, muscly length of his body. His erection presses into me. He is so hard and big.

Mindlessly I rub against his hardness. I'm filled with want. Want. Want. Want. I want to devour him. I want to scratch tracks down his back and tear out handfuls of his hair. I want to live in this intoxicating heat.

He breaks away, his lips seeking out my neck. Moaning, I tilt my head to give him easier access.

"Come home with me," he whispers, his hot breath tickling my skin before he starts kissing my neck again.

I can't locate the words to respond.

I don't want him to stop.

He lifts his head and kisses me again, deeper this time. My face is hot and I feel as if I'm ready to burst into flames.

"Come home with me," he repeats, lips moving over mine, hot breath mingling with mine.

I want this man the way I've never wanted anyone before. I want to fall into him, letting him take me where he wants to go. I've never wanted anything more than I want this, but I can't. "No," I whisper. "I have to get back for Janna. She can't wake up without me there."

He steps back, depriving me of the addictive heat and his musky, intoxicating smell. My fevered brain sees it as a kind of punishment. It takes all I have to keep from putting my hands on him again. I muss his hair and jerk the front of his shirt, nearly pulling it out of his pants.

For the first time, he doesn't look like he just stepped out of the pages of a men's magazine. Seeing him this way makes me want him even more. I sway, wanting to fall into his arms, but ...

Janna. I have to get home to Janna.

"I can have you home before morning," he says, purring the words in a luscious whisper.

He wants me as badly as I want him, but he's keeping his

distance, letting the heat rise between us, that sweet, painful need growing between my legs is unbearable.

"I can't," I whisper, and though his expression doesn't change I can see he is disappointed by the rigid set of his shoulders and his eyes. His eyes are always burning with need. Now that I know how hot he gets when we touch, and how good his body feels pressed into mine, how will I ever keep my hands off him?

His posture relaxes, giving a charming languidness to his long limbs. He runs a hand through his golden hair, smoothing back what I messed up in my frenzied need to touch him and eat him alive. He's closed up tight again, just that cool, handsome façade locking in whatever he's keeping from me.

"When can I see you again?" he asks softly.

"Tomorrow night." I'm desperate to see him again, even if I do think he's hiding something important behind an impenetrable wall of charm and smolder.

"I don't want to wait that long. Lunch?"

My shoulders droop with disappointment. I shake my head. "I'm sorry, I can't. I promised Janna we'd spend the day together tomorrow. We're going to the park."

He watches me for a long moment, his warm eyes cooling several degrees to meet the chilly temperature of the rest of his expression. "I'll meet you there."

"But I'll have Janna."

He shrugs. "I like kids."

"Okay," I say.

A genuinely warm smile pops onto his lips.

CHAPTER ELEVEN

RAVEN

*J*ust as I am about to fit my key into Bertha's door to get Janna, our front door opens and Cindy pops her head out.

"I've already got her," she says.

"Oh," I exclaim surprised, and walk towards her.

"Tell me everything!" she squeals, pulling me into our apartment. I'd lay bets that she watched from our window while Konstantin helped me out of his car and gave me another swoon-worthy kiss goodnight. Even though it was chaste compared to the ones on the patio, it was steamy as hell.

"What are you doing here? Aren't you supposed to be working until the morning," I ask.

"You expect me to stay on at the casino after Mark saw you leave the casino in a *Lambo*, Raven?" she asks in an impatient voice.

I shake my head at her. "So you just *left* work?"

She makes a dismissive gesture with one hand. "I haven't been sick for years. I was due a bit of time off so I faked a migraine and rushed home to hear all the details. I've been waiting for two fuckin' hours!"

I glance down the darkened hallway. "Did you see that Janna's missing a tooth?"

Her mouth opens. "She lost a tooth?"

"Apparently. Come on, let's go see."

We tiptoe down the corridor to Janna's room and like two fools crouch over her and carefully pull up her lip and gaze at the gap.

"Oh my god, how cute," Cindy whispers.

I look up at Cindy and grin, feeling weirdly proud. As if Janna has done something super amazing. I pull a five pound note out of my purse and stick it under her pillow. Bertha knows to save the tooth for me. I'm keeping them all in a jam jar until the sad day that Janna is old enough to learn that the tooth fairy doesn't exist.

We go back to the living room and I collapse on the couch, sighing as I think of a way to tell her about the events of the evening. I feel exhilarated and confused about it all.

She curls up next to me. "Well?"

"I don't even know where to start, Cin."

"From the beginning would be fine."

I start by telling her about the things that did not disorientate me or make me feel almost dizzy with excitement. Nothing like this has ever happened in my life before. The car. I tell her how intoxicating it was to have all that power rumbling underneath me.

She makes a rolling motion with her hand.

I take a deep breath and try to find words to describe my interaction with Konstantin. How, even though we barely spoke or made eye contact during the drive, I could feel the heat of our connection. I tell her about the tiny restaurant and the intensity of the make-out session on the patio. I tell her how he asked me to go home with him.

"I can still feel his hands on me," I whisper. I press my palms to my flaming cheeks. "When he starts kissing me, Cin, I don't ever want it to end. I've never felt this way about a man before."

She looks at me with even more disappointment than I feel. "What the hell are you doing here, then? Why didn't you go home with him?"

"I don't know, Cin."

"When was the last time you got some hmmm? Two years ago?"

"I was thinking of Janna."

"What? That's your excuse? You know Bertha or I would have watched her if you asked, especially if we knew you were finally going to get a bit of sex."

I frown and think about why I was sitting on the couch with Cindy and not having the most exciting sex I've known with Konstantin. I used Janna as the reason, but there's more to my refusal than that.

"The thing is … I don't know anything about him. He is so … mysterious. We had dinner together, I told him everything about me, and he practically told me nothing about himself. He's hiding something, Cindy. I have no reason for saying it and it sounds stupid, but I just feel it in my bones. And my gut is usually dead on." I chew my bottom lip. "I know it will sound totally mad to you, but I don't think he was at that party by accident."

"Thank god he was. Those guys would have really hurt you if he hadn't stepped in when he did."

I frown. "I know he definitely saved your necklace and probably my life too, but there's something about him, Cin. Something that makes me wary. I can't say why, but if I take away the burning attraction it's there the whole time."

"What do you mean?"

"There's a coldness to him."

"I didn't see anything cold about that kiss outside," Cindy says, grinning like the Cheshire cat.

"No, I'm not doing a good job of explaining this. It's not exactly coldness. It's like there's a blank wall and he's standing behind it. I can't explain it."

"Call me simple but here's my theory. He saw you at the party. Thought you were hot as hell and decided to follow you. He's a rich guy. Maybe the reason he seems so cold is because he doesn't want to commit. But then neither do you."

I fix my gaze on her. "The party was not the first time he saw me. He was at the casino before the party."

Cindy frowns. "What do you mean?"

"I saw him a few days earlier at one of the blackjack tables. He was dressed very casually and he was wearing a baseball cap, but I recognized him."

Cindy rises up and rests her temple on her fist. "Here's my take on all this. Don't overcomplicate it. A rich, intelligent, and insanely good-looking guy has the hots for you and you have the hots for him. Since he's obviously not dangerous, notice how many chances he's had to hurt you and hasn't taken the bait, I'm thinking you should give him a shot. Just have some fun. You don't have to marry him."

I look at her uncertainly.

"Look how many times we've seen really rich guys come and lose more than a million and what do they do? They don't bat an eyelid. Rich men are different and that's probably what you're feeling."

"What if he breaks my heart, Cin?"

She looks astonished. "What?"

I nod. "This guy could break my heart into a million pieces."

"You just met the guy, Raven."

"I know. I can't explain the way I feel about him. He just does something to me, you know."

"Right."

There is a moment of silence. "What would you do if you were me?"

"I'd go for it," she says immediately. "Even if I thought there was a one percent chance that it could work with a man like that I'd take it. He's just too special to give up without trying."

"You really think that?"

"Absolutely. If a guy like him wanted me I wouldn't hesitate. Not one second."

Konstantin's handsome face flashes into my mind ... those burning eyes.

"Are you going to see him again?" Cindy asks.

"Yeah," I say slowly. "I told him Janna and I would have lunch with him in the park tomorrow."

Cindy leaps up and coming over to me crushes me in a tight hug, rocking me back and forth the way we haven't since grade school. "I'm so happy for you, babe! So happy. It's been way too long since you had a man."

"I can't argue with that," I say with a laugh.

She leans away from me. "I know you think this is a bad idea, but I have a good feeling about this guy."

CHAPTER TWELVE

RAVEN

*I*t takes me a long time to fall asleep. When I do my sleep is restless. Full of strange dreams that don't make sense. I keep waking up to check the time. Finally, at three in the morning, I succumb to a deep slumber. Even then I dream.

I am at the casino and my sister is still alive. I'm unsurprised by the fact. She is wearing her favorite yellow dress and she is carrying Janna. There is no milk for Janna and I offer to go out and buy some. I walk towards the back entrance. I open the door and step into pitch blackness. I can hear the sound of something breathing heavily. Then I hear footsteps. Heavy. A man. His strides are slow and deliberate. I know that he is coming for me, but I am unable to run. My feet are rooted to the spot. I just stand there waiting for him to appear. He comes closer and closer …

I wake up with a start, drenched in a cold sweat.

What the hell was that dream about?

Breathing hard I turn to look at the clock. It is just after six-thirty. I untwist the blankets from my body and go to the bathroom to splash cold water on my face and change into a dry T-shirt. I don't hear Janna yet, so I pad over to her bedroom, needing her soft, innocent presence after such a terrifying nightmare. I like to bury my nose in her hair to breathe in the candy sweet scent of her shampoo. I open the door quietly and find her wide awake and flipping through the pages of her favorite book. She is actually reading to her toys.

"Mummy, you're awake!" she chirps happily, flashing the adorable gap in her teeth.

"Morning, sweets. I didn't know you were up."

"I am," she says, nodding vigorously, but she doesn't disentangle herself from her nest of stuffed toys and blankets. She likes to sleep with every soft toy she owns and as soon as she wakes up she always arranges them all around her.

"Why didn't you come to my bed?" I ask.

"Because Aunty Cindy says I'm not allowed to disturb you until the long hand touches twelve and the short hand touches seven on the clock," she explains solemnly.

I walk up to her bed and she moves some toys to make space for me. I bend down and pretend to look surprised. "My goodness! What happened to your tooth?"

"It fell out," she says touching the gap.

"Did you check under the pillow to see if the tooth fairy left you some money?"

Instantly, she dives under all her toys, and comes out beaming triumphantly and holding up my five-pound note. "Look, Mummy."

"Wow. What will you buy with it?"

"Is it enough for a pony?"

I raise my eyebrows. "Janna ..."

"All right," she sighs. "Is it enough for three ice creams?" She starts counting it out on her fingers. "One for you, and one for me, and one for Aunty Cindy, and one for nana, and one for gramps."

"That's five ice creams," I correct. I curl two of her fingers. "That's three and," I pull the other two out. "And that's five."

"Is it enough for five ice creams?"

I nod and smile. "Yes, my darling. That is enough money for all of us. It's very generous of you to share."

"Can we have it for breakfast?"

"No, we don't have ice cream for breakfast, but guess what?"

Her eyes become round. "What?"

"We're doing something very special this afternoon."

She sits up, tiny fingers giving a good scratch to the back of her head, her curls bobbing over her shoulders. The ends are a bit straggly and she needs a haircut, but I can't bear to let anyone put scissors to all those sweet curls.

"I made a new friend and he wants to meet you."

"Is your friend a pony?"

"No. It's a man."

"Oh, okay," she says with a shrug.

I have to laugh. To me, Konstantin is a force of nature, an earthshattering development that has turned my life upside down. But Janna couldn't care less. She'd exchange him for a pony any day.

I open my arms and she launches herself with the force of a small torpedo into me, nearly knocking me backwards onto the floor.

"I love you, little munchkin," I whisper into her sweet-smelling hair. I close my eyes and take a deep breath. Whenever I say those words aloud to Janna, I say it in my heart to Octavia too. I pull back. "Now let's get some breakfast. We're having pancakes."

"Yay!"

※

We couldn't have chosen a more perfect day to have lunch in the park. It's warm, the sun beats down on our shoulders when we step off of the bus. I keep Janna's tiny, sweaty hand in mine as we walk from the bus stop, across the street, and into the park. My eyes scan the street, but I don't see Konstantin's Lamborghini lurking anywhere.

Maybe he'll stand us up.

My stomach is in knots. I can't decide whether that would be better than finding him waiting for us. I don't know what I was thinking bringing Janna along. She's become excited to meet my *special friend*. I hope I'm not making a big mistake.

I told Konstantin we'd wait for him in the center of the park near the ice cream van. Janna and I come here often so she can run herself ragged on the playground and have an ice cream before going home to crash for an hour or two.

"I wanna swing!" Janna screeches, tugging hard on my arm with the full weight of her compact body. She likes to pick her own clothes and her favorite is to wear clashing colors, but I strongly suggested she choose a matching outfit today —her favorite frilly skirt and sky blue t-shirt.

I've dressed a little better than I usually would for an afternoon at the park too. I'm wearing a pair of skinny jeans and a silky blue tank top that makes my eyes pop. I made a real effort with my hair too, sweeping the bulk of my hair back into a fashionably messy ponytail.

I spot Konstantin before he sees us. He is sitting on a bench watching the kids on the playground. He looks relaxed in an olive-green shirt, open at the collar, and faded blue jeans. I feel a warm thrill to find him waiting here for me. Early is good. It means he is as eager as I am.

He turns as we approach, but doesn't stand, just watches me with those smoking eyes. All the heat from the night before comes flooding back and all those aching, needy places inside me start throbbing for him. Thank God I have Janna to focus on now.

"Janna, this is my friend, Konstantin," I say, letting go of her hand.

"Hello, Janna," he says, smiling gently.

"Hi," she says. Before Konstantin can respond again, she scurries up into his lap, moving so quickly, I can't catch hold of her shoulder to keep her from climbing up there.

"Janna!" I whisper, horrified. She has never done that to a stranger before.

She completely ignores me and he leans back to give her room to get comfortable, but doesn't seem to mind having her in his lap. She stares up at him openly, grinning hard and showing off her missing tooth. That kid can—and does—get away with just about anything after flashing a smile like that.

She lifts her chin and smooths her hair back. "If you want you can be my daddy."

I redden to the roots of my hair. To Konstantin's credit, he doesn't flinch, doesn't lose the serene smile he's giving Janna, who's staring up at him like he's the most beautiful thing she's ever seen. I know how she feels.

"Oh," I mumble, trying for a smile, but failing miserably, "I'm sorry. All her friends at playschool have daddies and she wants one too." I want to snatch her off his lap before she says something else equally embarrassing, but the little madam has snuggled happily into his chest. It's strange to see her doing that because she's never so forward with complete strangers. Overall, she's a happy, friendly kid, but she always keeps her distance when she first meets someone. I guess I have never introduced her to a man friend before so I never knew how she would react.

"It's fine," he says, his eyes flicking up to my face. His mouth curves into a carefree grin that makes me want to lick his mouth. Before I move on to licking other things. My scalp prickles as my blush moves past my hairline.

"I like your hair," Janna says, peering up at Konstantin, who has to tuck his chin in drastically in order to look down at her.

"What do you like about it?" he asks. There's a sweetness to his voice that I haven't heard before. It's usually rigidly held, cautious, mostly devoid of emotion, and accentless, which is why it was so surprising to hear him speak another language to the waiter last night. The mysteriousness that surrounds him seems to indicate that he has no past at all, as though he simply appeared out of thin air exactly as I see him now.

"It's yellow," she says. "Like the prince in my story. If you marry my mummy, she'll be a princess."

"Janna. Stop being so rude."

She turns towards me. "I'm not being rude, Mummy." She turns away from me and looks at Konstantin. "Am I being rude?"

He shakes his head quickly. "No."

She turns back to me. "See."

"It's rude to ask people personal questions," I say sternly, and with my eyes widened and staring at her. She knows what that means. Wait till I get you home!

She decides to ignore me. "Do you live in a castle?"

Konstantin glances up at me, his lips pursed to hold back a smile, "No," he says to her.

"Oh," she says, disappointed.

"Do you want a hotdog, Janna?" I say loudly. "You can play on the swings after you eat. And have an ice cream. Would you like that?"

Nodding, she detaches herself from Konstantin and hops back onto the ground. He rises from the bench, shifting the dynamic. I look up at him and his eyes are hotter than I've ever seen them. It is just that easy for him to turn on the electricity. I feel that zapping energy running up my arms, my legs, down my spine. I pointedly glance away from him, take Janna by the hand, and lead her towards the hotdog vendor while Konstantin follows closely behind.

We order hotdogs and bottled water, all Konstantin's treat, then find a shady spot beneath a tree to lay down the blanket I brought and eat our lunch. We've wandered away from the noise on the playground, though that keeps attracting the better part of Janna's attention. With the cool breeze and chilled water to drink, it's actually quite comfortable in the shade.

Janna wolfs down her hotdog, smearing ketchup all over her face. I wipe it off with a wet wipe while Konstantin looks on, his head tilted to one side as if the domesticity of the scene intrigues and surprises him.

Konstantin eats quickly as well, not saying a word unless it's in response to one of Janna's direct questions. She clearly likes him a great deal. The detached chilliness of his expression has melted away a little. His eyes are animated and engaged instead of just alternating between wary and hot. Janna's a good influence on him and vice versa. Maybe this wasn't such a bad idea after all.

Eating seems to relax us. It worked the same way last night. Janna lays back on the blanket to count the leaves on the maze of thick branches above our heads, extending a chubby index finger to mark each one.

The shade, the gentle breeze, the sound of Janna's murmured counting—it's perfect. Not to mention the musky scent of Konstantin on the breeze that floats down to me. We're extremely close to one another. If I leaned a few inches to the left, I'd be resting on his shoulder.

Janna's counting is slowing down. Yawning, she lowers her arm but keeps up the tally, valiantly fighting a battle she slowly loses each day around this time, her little body eventually succumbing to the drag of sleep.

Konstantin's fingers run slowly up my arm from my elbow to just below my shoulder.

Shivering, I swallow back a moan before turning to meet his eyes. The expression in them takes my breath away.

"She's a sweet kid," he whispers.

My heart's thundering in my chest as the blood rushes up to my head.

"You're good with her." It's a struggle to keep my voice from wavering. I feel sixteen around him, which both thrills and annoys me. I'm twenty-three, playing mother and holding down a full-time job, not some silly, love-struck kid. And yet, to feel this way again …

"She's good with me, you mean," he teases, with a gentle laugh.

"Do you have brothers and sisters?"

"I had siblings." He doesn't elaborate. Had? I look into his eyes and already the shutters are back down. That makes three things I know about him now. Except I don't actually know what type of business he's in. I also don't know how many siblings he had and how he lost them.

Of course, I also have absolutely no idea how old he is. His detached, mysterious demeanor makes him seem years older than I am, decades even, but that's not possible. His finely formed features are blemish and wrinkle free. He can't be more than a few years older than me. I'd be surprised to learn he's much more than thirty.

I watch him closely for a moment, but he's looking past me at Janna, his eyes unreadable. When he looks at me again, his eyes have morphed once more. They've become hotter. The air is suddenly much too heavy to breathe. I'm sweaty all over.

He touches my arm again, his fingers lingering on the soft skin on the inside of my wrist. An invitation. I lean closer, then shake my head.

"Not with Janna here ..."

"She's sleeping," he whispers, his voice hoarse.

In the brief second it takes to confirm that Janna is indeed snoozing on the blanket next to me, Konstantin has scooted closer. His face is only inches away from mine. Those shapely lips come together and a burst of his hot breath ignites my skin. I can't resist him.

I move the inch and press my mouth to his, pushing my tongue past his lips, wanting to taste him, to get at that heat that animates his amazing eyes. Primitive need rushes up from between my legs. We're in the middle of a public park surrounded by children, but I can't stop. I don't fight him when he pulls me roughly over to him. I straddle his legs. I can feel how much he wants me. I move my crotch over that thick hardness between us, moaning as he ravages my mouth with his.

I pull away from him, breathless.

"I have to get to work," I gasp.

He grabs my hips and grinds me on his cock, drawing a moan from me.

"When can I see you again?" he asks.

I can't look away from his eyes. In the shade, they look almost black.

"Whenever you want," I say hoarsely.

"Tonight?"

"Yes," I whisper, still rocking in his lap as he guides my hips. I want to mess up his hair by running my hands through it. I want to kiss him until our mouths bleed. I want to tear his clothes off and climb onto his lap and ride him until we come in a frenzy of pleasure and agony.

"I'll wait for you outside the casino. What time do you finish?" He kisses me again, but not deeply, just enough to get my hips going again. I swear, if I didn't have Janna here, I'd find a secluded spot, slip out of my wet panties, and ride him for real.

"My shift ends at eleven," I say.

He leans into my neck, kissing a trail up to my ear. "I'm going to fuck you until you scream. Tell me you want that."

I answer him in a breathless whisper. "God, yes."

He laughs into my neck, a low triumphant sound. "And so you shall be."

CHAPTER THIRTEEN

RAVEN

https://www.youtube.com/watch?v=NwL98zzdEXo
(Can you blow my whistle, baby?)

*M*y heart flutters as Konstantin's Lamborghini races through the streets of London. I haven't slept with a man in years. Even before Octavia passed I had already begun to spend all of my free time at her place, both to help with Janna and to care for my sister. Of course, after she died, my focus turned exclusively to Janna.

I haven't found a reason to seek out a man … until now.

We cross the Thames river at Embankment and Konstantin takes us down quiet streets. I watch his hands as they steer the car with complete confidence. Mine are clenched tightly in my lap. He hooks a hard right into the underground garage of an impressive apartment building.

Konstantin parks the car, gets out, and comes around to help me out. Taking my hand, he leads me into the building. He's barely spoken to me since I came out of the casino to find him resting against his car, dressed in a finely cut suit that perfectly accented his broad shoulders, long legs, and trim, muscular torso. My first thought: none of it is staying long on his body. This time when I sit on his lap, I don't want a single stitch between us.

He glances down at me in the lift. "You okay?"

My mouth goes dry at the expression in his eyes. I nod and we say nothing else. His apartment is only a few floors up.

He unlocks his door and steps aside to let me into the filmy darkness first. As I venture inside, he turns on the lights. It's very … um … modern and sparse to the point of clinical. Lots of gleaming metal and nothing by way of decoration at all. It's as if he has just moved in, only there are no boxes lying around waiting to be unpacked.

By contrast our apartment is full of photos of the three of us laughing, cheap paintings, fridge magnets, rugs, magazines, color, toys, mess. All our personalities, even little Janna's, are everywhere. Here, there is not a single personal touch of the owner. Two expensive black leather couches form a corner. In between is a deep-brown leather coffee table, designer obviously.

Carefully color-matched modern paintings adorn the wall. Except for the one that boasts a large flat screen television. To the left of it is a glass and burnished copper drinks bar that just screams handcrafted. Further into the open plan space is the dining table, another polished glass, leather and chrome affair. It is impossible to think of Konstantin sitting there having a meal with friends.

It is one of those perfectly coordinated lifestyle homes that look as if every item in it was bought at one time by a professional, and without love. The far wall is pure glass, giving a fabulous view of the city lights beyond the river. I don't even want to know what it costs to rent such a place.

"Would you like a drink?" he asks.

I turn around. He has wandered over to the beverage cart while I was taking inventory of his impressive, but cold apartment. Even the air is a few degrees colder in here than it was outside. The place is an accurate mirror of the façade he shows the world. An armor that is undeniably beautiful, but inhospitable and unwelcoming.

"Sure," I say, matching his tone.

"What would you like?"

"Whatever you're having is fine."

"Dry Martini?"

I've never had it before. "Great."

"Have a seat."

I walk over to the couch and perch at the end.

I watch him make the drinks and pour the mixture out into two glasses. He crosses the room, hands one to me, and sits beside me. When he sets his drink on the leather coffee table and turns to me, I react by taking the cocktail stick with the olive out, and downing my entire drink in two swallows. It's strong as hell. I'm so nervous my hands are shaking.

He smiles at my empty glass. "Nervous?"

I shrug one shoulder. "A bit."

"No need. We both know how this plays out." He takes the empty glass from my nerveless fingers and puts it on the table along with his untouched drink. Then he scoots closer.

I pop the olive into my mouth and chew it. I showered, shaved, rubbed lotion on my whole body, and chose my cutest thong underwear, but I still feel like a fraud. A man like him, who lives in an apartment like this. What the hell is he doing with me?

He draws me into a tender kiss, his tongue only playing this time instead of forcing its way inside. He pulls me more tightly into him, one hand at the back of my neck while the other takes gentle hold of one knee and begins to move it steadily away from my other. The hunger rises inside me.

"You're so fucking beautiful," he whispers, lips on my lips so I'm breathing in his words.

I start unbuttoning his shirt, but he shakes his head, a mysterious smile on his lips. "Not yet. He trails his fingers along my inner thigh. "I want you to strip for me."

My eyes widen. "You mean like a striptease?"

"No. A striptease is performed to titillate a man. I'm so titillated I'm bursting out of my pants. Just stand in front of me and take your clothes off. Everything but your shoes."

I stand and walk around the coffee table. I don't feel confident about my body, but the magnetic hold he seems to have over me and the molten lust in his eyes makes me brave. Slowly, I unzip the sexy cerise dress I changed into at the casino. Cindy and I chose it together. Actually, Cindy chose it. I thought it was too risqué. She said it was perfect. I let it slide down my body and pool around my shoes.

He leans back, and never taking his eyes off me, reaches for his drink. He takes a sip and I unclasp my bra. He inhales sharply as the material falls away and my breasts are exposed. Hooking my fingers into the material of my panties,

I slowly slide them down my thighs. His eyes feast hungrily on my freshly shaved pussy. I had ruined the landing strip so I just shaved everything off. His eyes rise up to meet mine.

"Turn around. I want to see your ass."

My knees are wobbly as I swivel.

"Part your legs."

I close my eyes. I am so wet, my juices are soaking my inner thighs. I widen my stance. If I open my legs, he'll see the trails.

"A bit more," his voice rings out.

I obey.

"Bend over."

I hesitate for a moment. I've never done this for any man. Then, slowly I lean forward and expose my swollen glistening flesh to him.

"Let your palms touch the floor."

I drop down. I can see him from between my legs.

The only sound in the room for a few minutes is our strained breathing. More lubrication slides down my legs almost reaching my knees.

He stands and walks up to me. He is so close I can feel the heat from his body. All I can see are his fully clothed legs. It is strangely erotic that I am completely naked and he is fully dressed.

His finger follows the wet trails. That tiny, feather-light contact with his skin makes me moan. He slides his finger around on the slick moisture.

"Did you think of me and make yourself cum in the last few days?" he asks softly.

I nod.

"I can't hear you, baby."

"Yes." My voice is so soft. It is almost a whisper.

"Is your pussy big enough for my cock, little Raven?"

I shiver with need. "Yes."

He inserts a long finger into me, making my knees buckle. He twists the finger sensuously inside me as I bite my lip to stop from crying out. Without warning, he wraps his arm around my waist, pulls me upright, and twirls me around. I stare up at him, my eyes wide with surprise and excitement. He holds his wet finger in front of my lips. An inch away, but not touching.

His eyes are heavy lidded and dark with desire. "Suck."

I lean forward and slowly, seductively, suck his finger into my mouth. Something flares up in his eyes. The incredible ferocity of it shocks me. Surely such lust is insanity. We stare at each other in disbelief. My entire mind feels clouded by desire. He grabs my shoulders, pushes me to my knees.

I look up at him and he takes my chin in his hand and looks down at me, an indecipherable expression on his face.

"What?" I whisper.

He turns his head and looks at the couch next to the one we were sitting on. I follow his gaze and freeze. I never saw it. I can't. I can't do that.

"Don't you want to see how sexy you look with my cock buried in your mouth, baby."

If any other man had asked me that question I would have slapped him hard, but with him everything I know about myself is turned upside down. He alone ignites such wanton desires and wild abandonment in my rational practical mind it is shocking. I do want to see what I look like with his cock in my mouth.

I nod and he picks up the video camera and points it down at me. For a second I am paralyzed, then I lift my hands and undo his belt buckle while he watches me from behind the recording equipment.

His trousers fall down his slim hips and I see his cock, thick, hard and massive. The desire to touch it and taste it fills me and I practically rip his underwear off and yank them down to his knees. His cock springs free and I caress the hard shaft. The skin under my fingers is warm and as silky as satin.

"Good girl," he encourages softly.

CHAPTER FOURTEEN

KONSTANTIN

https://www.youtube.com/watch?v=zFGqpeJltBk
(Never Known A Girl Like You Before)

I take her chin and bring her open mouth to the tip of my cock. Her eyes swivel up to watch me looking down at her through the lens of the video camera, before going back to staring at my cock with an intensity I've never seen before. Her nipples are hard and her face is flushed with excitement. She extends her tongue, licks the tip, then looks up at me again. She has no idea how absolutely beautiful she looks.

"Don't stop, sweetheart."

She opens those crazy-sexy lips, stretches them around my thickness, and takes me inside. Fuck, I'm barely in that hot wet mouth and I almost lose it. Closing her eyes to fully savor my cock, she starts slowly sucking me in. Every few seconds she bobs deeper until she has about half of my dick in her mouth.

I feel the head push against her throat, but that's just the beginning of the show. No gagging. No panicked requests not to come in her mouth. No, I-just-need-a-minute-to-catch-my-breath. Instead, she keeps on steadily sliding down the shaft, until my entire cock disappears into her face, and her lips are sealed around the base of my cock. Every inch of my cock is inside her silky mouth. To prove it the tip of her tongue licks against my balls.

Jesus! I was right. Little Miss Innocent is a secret slut.

I watch her wait silently without the ability to breathe in that pose of complete submission, almost worship, and hell, I almost come right there and then. I withdraw from her throat to cool myself down and allow her to breathe. In the view finder through which I watch the scene unfolding before me, my cock seems incredibly big, thick, and glistening with saliva as it flows out of her plump mouth.

I watch her take a deep breath then instantly swallow my cock whole again, her lips sinking all the way down to the base. God, she is perfect. She repeats her clever trick again and again. Every time she sucks me back in she does it as if she can't get enough of my cock. I grunt with pleasure as she works her slow, sure magic.

Pressing her tongue hard against the underside of my cock she begins to hum. The vibrations go right through me, my entire body tingles, and my mind goes blank with insane pleasure.

Fucking amazing technique that, but is she always like this? So eager for a man's cock? Who taught her to deep throat? How many dicks has she taken into that red mouth? The thoughts burn my gut in a way that is totally unfamiliar. Insane with lust and jealous rage, I throw the video camera to the couch and roughly grab a handful of her hair.

Her blue eyes fly open. There is excitement but also a touch of fear.

Tightening my grip on her silky hair I plunge my dick deep into her wet throat. Automatically she angles her throat to allow me full access. I thrust in and out. Her fingers dig into my hips for support and she moans loudly, but not once does she resist. In fact, she keeps her head still as I fuck her mouth.

The sound of my cock in her hot, moist throat fills the room and I explode, pumping hot cum down her throat. I withdraw slightly and watch her mouth fill with my semen. She swallows every drop. My hips continue making little jerking pushes with each shot until my still-hard cock slides out of her throat. Softly, she licks the head of my cock, cleaning the last of my seed.

Her gentle licking prevents me from going soft, and soon I'm hard again.

She stays on her knees, panting heavily, her thighs clenched hard, and her eyes pleading.

"Fuck me … please fuck me! I need you inside me," she whispers.

My cock throbs at her words. I roll on a condom, grab her under her arms and lift her up, holding her steady. I take one of her legs and lift it up, opening her dripping pussy. She wraps her legs around my waist, and the spiky heels of her sexy shoes dig into my flesh.

I press my cock against her open pussy and she gasps with

anticipation. Holding it there for just a second, I enjoy the sensation of her juices sliding down my cock, her frustration. Watching her expression, I press my length into her. Hell, she wasn't lying when she said it has been years since she was with a man. Even dripping wet, I have to push hard with my hips to stretch her open.

She's so hot and so wet and so tight it feels fantastic. Her pussy walls pulse and tremble around my cock. Halfway in, I slowly pull back out until my cock head reaches her opening, then I thrust in again hard, making her grunt.

With each thrust I force more and more into her until I look down, and I have bottomed out. My entire cock enters her completely with each stroke. Her breath comes out ragged and hoarse.

I pull her close to me, press my lips to her and say the most surprising thing. "You're mine. Every fucking inch of you is mine."

The sound is torn from her mouth. "Yes. Every inch."

Her breath is warm against my cheek. I fuck her hard then. Mindlessly pounding into her. There is no thought in my head. All I want to do is fuck. Her.

At one point I bite her throat, and she comes hard around my cock, her head thrown back, her body arching, contracting and shaking uncontrollably. The sight thrills me the way nothing else has. She's *mine*. My sex toy. To do with as I please. I fucking own her.

Like a caveman I fill her tight little pussy with my hard cock, again and again. With every thrust I tell her that she belongs to me. Her body is mine. Her cunt is mine. She gasps, "Yes, oh God, yes."

As I skim the edge of my own release, I see her body begin to tighten again so I wait for her. Climax comes to her like a lightning bolt of pleasure. She goes rigid, her mouth open in a silent scream, then she loses all muscle control. I grip her tightly and let myself finally come. Fuck, it hits me so hard I feel almost dizzy.

I'm still holding her in a death grip. I move my body back and look at her. Her mouth is swollen, her breasts are rosy, and my cock is still buried inside her. I take my hand away from her ribs and see the bruises that have already started to form where I've held her so forcefully and where I've bitten her. Fascinated, I reach out and stroke the darkening skin.

"I've marked you," I note, but my voice is possessive and unapologetic.

She looks down. "It's all right, I bruise easily," she dismisses.

I look into her eyes. "I enjoyed leaving my mark on your body."

She stares at me. "Then leave more."

I smile slowly.

"My oh my, oh my. You're becoming hard again," she murmurs in wonder.

I pull out of her and roll on a fresh condom. "Come here."

She doesn't need a second invitation. She steps up to me, cocks her leg around my body and, impaling her wet pussy on my shaft, begins to thrust her hips. Sliding the swollen flesh up and down my cock, she moans softly every time her clit grinds against me.

I lift her off the ground, and she wraps her legs around my back and throws her arms around my neck.

"I've never been with a man like you. It feels like you belong inside my body," she whispers in my ear.

With our bodies joined, I walk her to the bedroom and sit on the bed. She straddles me, my cock buried deep inside her. Her mouth finds mine. Soft and wet. She makes me *forget*. She is the first woman who has been able to do that. Slowly, with my tongue in her mouth, she rises and drops herself on my length, gently at first, but in no time she is humping me for all she's worth.

Her body is slick with sweat and her round, full breasts bounce wildly. I bite one of her nipples, and she throws her head back and lets out a low cry. I suck the stinging bud. Completely lost in pleasure her body starts shaking.

"Look at me, Raven," I order.

She brings her head forward and tries to focus on my face.

"Go on. I want to watch you come." I move back a little and look at her, naked and beautiful, break apart on my cock. With her hips jerking, her mouth open in a shrill scream, her entire body shuddering, and tears running down her face. I hold her firm ass in my hands and enjoy the exciting sensation of having a woman completely lose it on my cock.

CHAPTER FIFTEEN

RAVEN

*H*e gets on his elbows and gazes down at me, his bright eyes casting a spell I can't break, not that I want to.

"Come away with me," he says softly.

"Me? Away?" I'm so drunk on him I can't even string a coherent sentence together. It could be from the shock of suddenly ending a complete and utter sex deprivation, or from how earth-shattering sex has just been. Most probably a combination of both.

He leans forward to touch my lips with his. A chaste kiss that is somehow more erotic than all the deeper ones. He speaks over my mouth, the words forming on both our lips at once.

"I know a place in the country. It is quiet and remote. We would be alone. All day and all night."

All day and all night! God, there is nothing I want more. I crave this man like he is some kind of drug. His cool demeanor draws me in instead of doing the opposite. It's his eyes. The heat in them, and the need that sizzles my insides.

"We could leave anytime you like. Tomorrow? Tonight?"

Now it's my turn to laugh, but weakly. Escaping into the night with him sounds like the craziest best idea in the world. He stares at me.

"I can't just leave town at the drop of a hat."

"Why not?"

For a few seconds I can't remember why not either.

Yes, of course. My job. My responsibilities. The people who depend on me. Although, to be perfectly honest, at this moment, with his steady heartbeat matching my own, everyone else can go to hell … except I'm bound to my little munchkin. I can't just disappear on her to run off with some guy who knows how to hypnotize with his eyes and his cock.

"It won't be for long," he cajoles. He kisses the tip of my nose, my chin, my forehead, all the while, the full length of his powerful, well-built body is pressing into mine.

I moan, running my hands down his back, fingers reaching to caress the curve of his firm buttocks.

"How about this weekend? I promise you will not regret saying yes." He presses his hips into mine. Jesus! He's hard again.

"I have to work this weekend."

I can't stop running my hands over him. I feel the electricity living in his skin snap at my fingertips. I can't believe I've been missing out on this for all these years. I don't regret focusing on Janna, but hell, I need this too.

He grinds his erection into me and I groan and wriggle invitingly. When he does that I find it impossible to think.

He moves to my neck, sucking lightly, not deterred in the slightest by all of my perfectly legitimate excuses. I want to go, but how can I leave Janna so suddenly?

"Think about it before you say no," he murmurs, mouth just below my ear, hot breath setting me aflame.

"I really ... really ... ah ... don't want to ... ah ... say no, but ... I've never ... ah ... left Janna for a whole ... oh God ... weekend."

He sucks my nipple. "What was it you said again?"

"I ... oh ... yes ... no. No, I can't leave Janna," I croak.

He lifts his gorgeous head, searing me with his eyes. "Is there no one else who can take care of her for the weekend?"

"I've never left her alone before."

"Can your flatmate not take care of her? What's her name?"

"Cindy," I supply.

"I'm happy to pay her if she'll agree to do it. Ask her to name her price."

My eyes widen. "She won't want money."

He stares at me, his eyes blazing with frustration. "Won't you at least try to find someone to take care of her? Your parents perhaps?"

"Okay, I'll try," I whisper, not wanting to break the spell of this closeness by disappointing him, even though I know I can't go. I want to stay wrapped in this cocoon of his skin and heat for the rest of my life. To think I didn't even know this man last week.

Now I think I might be falling for him.

a text from Cindy is waiting for me when I get home from Konstantin's at nearly four in the morning and dawn is already in the sky.

Call me the minute you get home. I don't care how late it is. I want to know EVERYTHING.

I smile and let myself into Bertha's apartment. As I carry Janna back to our home, I feel a small stab of guilt at how much I wanted to leave her and go with Konstantin. My whole attention is no longer on her.

But that's silly.

None of these recent developments have kept me away from her any more than work already has. She would have been asleep even if I had come straight home from work. Still, I don't feel any better. I can't help how thoughts of him creep up on me in the middle of whatever I'm doing. In the soft morning light this new preoccupation that borders on downright obsession doesn't feel fair for her. She is just a child.

"I'll do better," I whisper to the snoozing small shape. "Promise."

In my room, I strip off the clothes that smell of Konstantin, and climb into bed. I don't really have the energy to call Cindy—I'm physically and emotionally spent after what

Konstantin and I did—but she will hunt me down tomorrow if I blow her off.

Yawning, I dial her.

"Raven?" she says crisply.

"You said to call," I say, sounding fuzzy.

"Did you just get home?"

"Yeah."

"It's past four in the morning. Damn, girl, have you been greasing his pole all this time?"

I can't help the smile that springs to my lips. I close my eyes so I can more clearly picture Konstantin's finely-formed, muscular physique. I could tell he had a nice body when he was fully clothed, but, goddamn, it still took me by complete surprise to actually have him standing naked in front of me the first time. Those tattoos that covered one arm and shoulder, flowing down and over his pecs.

I giggle. "That's an understatement."

"Did you use the deep throat techniques I taught you?"

"Of course."

"Are you now grateful for all that time I forced you to choke on the dildo?"

"You were right. It was worth every second," I concede.

"Good. Now that we have established the gratitude that is rightfully mine, I. Want. Every. Detail," she says, emphasizing each word while simultaneously doubling the space between them.

"I don't even know where to start. I've just never met anyone like him before, Cin. He's so different." I pause to force my racing thoughts into an idea that might make sense to her. How can I explain the incredible heat between us?

"What do you mean by different?"

"Everything with him is so hidden, but so hot, and so ... ugh. I can't explain it. He's like a deliciously muscular enigma. Did *you* notice anything about him that night at the casino when you took over my table?"

Cindy takes a few moments to answer, and I can see her chewing her lip as she thinks. "He was an expensively dressed, extremely handsome man who took the trouble to be charming, but was so reserved. To the point of appearing cold. I swear even the air around him was a couple of degrees colder. I certainly didn't see any of that heat you're talking about. He must save all the sexy stuff for you."

The thought—that maybe he can't control that smolder when I'm around, that maybe it just gets away from him—thrills me completely. I know how powerful his effect is on me, but it never occurred to me I might be casting the same spell on him. It seems incredible to think anything could get under that cool, collected façade.

"I think I'm falling for him." I admit it to myself and Cindy at the same time, which is how I make the better part of my breakthroughs. "I don't even know how you can fall for a guy you barely know anything about, but I am. I can't stop thinking about him, Cin. He asked me to go away with him to the country and it took everything I had not to immediately agree to go with him. If he'd asked me again, I'd probably have said yes."

Cindy sucks in a shocked breath, and I prepare myself: a lecture is on its way. "What? This gorgeous god of a man asked you to go away with him and you refused? Why? Why aren't you going on this trip?"

"You know why."

"Janna?" Her dry tone is like an accusatory finger poking into my chest.

"I can't just leave her alone for days at a time," I defend hotly.

"Let's conveniently forget that I'm around and I've helped out with Janna so often in the past I might as well be her second mother." She takes another deep breath. Really, she wants to shake me. "For God's sake, Raven. Sometimes the way you go on it's like you'll be leaving her to fend for herself in the streets."

"What about—"

"Work?" Cindy finishes. "I'll sort something out with Dave. You need this, Raven. After that horrible year with Octavia. You bloody well deserve this."

"I want to go, but …"

"So just go. You know you'll regret it if you don't."

It's a waste of time to try to argue with someone who's known you since you were a kid. I don't have any tricks that she hasn't seen a thousand times. That, of course, works both ways.

I sigh, long and drawn out.

"Come on. This will be good for you. You have to get out there and start living again. Stop using Janna as an excuse." When I don't answer, she continues in a gentler tone. "If you're happy, Janna will be happy too."

I don't answer her.

"What would Octavia tell you to do?"

I squeeze my eyes shut at the mention of poor, shrunken Octavia.

"He's hot. He likes you. You like him. Janna likes him. What's the problem?" she asks.

"I'm scared," I whisper. "I don't know anything about him. What if he hurts me?"

"You'll pick yourself up, dust yourself off and go on like all the rest of us."

I swallow hard. I've never been a coward before. "Okay. I'll go."

Cindy lets loose a celebratory whoop into the phone. "Yes!"

I have to laugh at how excited she is for me.

"Cin?"

"Yeah?"

"Thank you for being such an amazing friend."

"Talking of amazing friends. What are you doing tomorrow for lunch?"

"Nothing. Why?"

"Want to do lunch with Rosa tomorrow?" she asks.

I've already said I'm doing nothing so it's too late to back off. "What about Janna?"

"She'll come with us, obviously."

"All right," I say without any excitement in my voice.

She ignores my dull tone. "Great. Will you make sure I'm awake by 12.30 tomorrow?"

"I'll set Janna on you?"

"God no. Yesterday she launched herself into my bed so hard I've got a bruise the size of England on my side."

"Sorry. I'll have to warn her."

"Don't you dare. I love having her in my bed. It will be no time before she won't want to do that anymore."

I smile. "Okay."

"By the way. Why did you tell her that you were okay with her getting a pony if I was?"

I start laughing. "She's playing you, Cin."

"Ooo … the manipulative little minx," she says with a laugh. "Anyway, got to go."

We say goodnight and I start typing a text to Konstantin.

I'm good for the weekend in the country if the offer still stands.

I delete that. That sounds way too needy.

I'm available this weekend.

I delete that. Maybe something cheeky?

I'm up for that dirty weekend if you are.

With a grimace, I delete that too. I'll just keep it simple.

Do you still want to do that weekend away?

I don't expect to hear back from him right away. That's just how guys operate, not to mention he's way too mysterious and remote for a prompt reply. So, I'm pretty surprised to receive a response immediately.

I will prepare everything for this weekend. I cannot wait to be inside you again.

That heat washes over me as a blush blooms in my cheeks. I think of him in his nearly empty apartment, probably in bed. Naked. Those hot eyes that drive me crazy closed. I think about my conversation with Cindy and try on some of her confidence when I send my reply.

I'm excited too. x

He doesn't text back. I put my phone down, still flushed and lightheaded, and I snuggle deeper into my blankets, thinking about Konstantin and how good we were together.

CHAPTER SIXTEEN

RAVEN

*J*anna appears in the kitchen wearing a green T-shirt with the words CUTIE written in yellow, pink jeans, blue headband, and red shoes. Hooked under her elbow is her sparkly Barbie handbag. I happen to know that inside it she keeps a piece of purple string, a seashell she found on Brighton beach, an orange eraser, a ring with three random keys, and a mini plastic comb that came with her doll set.

"Why, Janna, you look beautiful," I say with a smile.

"I know," she says confidently and parks herself on a chair at the breakfast bar in our kitchen. She looks at me with considering eyes. "Why don't you wear what you wore to the park the other day, Mummy?"

"I can't wear the same thing all the time."

"But I like it when you look nice."

"Well, we're just going to see an old friend today. Nobody will be dressed up."

"I am."

I hide my smile. "The adults won't be. Now go get Aunty Cindy, please."

"No need. Here I am," Cindy says, coming out of her bedroom.

Even though she has only slept for three hours, she looks as fresh as a daisy.

"My goodness me, you look lovely, Janna," she says.

"Thank you," Janna says smugly.

"Right, are we all ready to go?"

"Yay! Chicken satay and fried ice cream," Janna shouts.

We get into a taxi and arrive at the restaurant in less than half-an-hour. Inside it is lovely and cool. A smiling woman shows us to our seats. Just as we are given our menus, I look up and see Star walking towards us. That same man with the earpiece is right behind her. For a second I am too astonished to do anything. Then I am filled with anger at Cindy's betrayal. I turn towards her furiously.

"How could you?"

She begs me with her eyes. "Come on," she pleads. "Just give her one chance."

I stand up. "No."

She stands too. "Please, Raven. What harm can it do to just hear her out?"

I look at Janna. She's looking at us with confusion. She has never seen us argue or fight before.

"Please, Raven. I'll take Janna for a walk. When you've finished talking, give me a ring and I'll bring her back."

Star arrives at our table. She is glowing with beauty. In a class poll she was voted most likely to marry a Prince or Billionaire. I was most likely to be a glamor model or porn star because I was an early developer and had bigger breasts than all the other girls. Rosa was most likely to be a CEO and Cindy was voted DJ material because she had such a big collection of music. Well, they were right about Star, anyway. She gazes at me. So much time has passed. Her eyes are different. She is not the girl I once knew. I guess we've all grown up.

"Come on, Raven," Cindy pleads.

I shake my head.

"I know I don't deserve it, but please, just give me a few minutes of your time. Please," Star says quietly.

At that moment, Rosa walks through the door.

I feel outgunned. "I don't—"

"Just listen to what she has to say, Raven. Rosa and I will take Janna down the street," Cindy says, and I realize I don't want Janna to see any of this.

"All right," I say, turning towards Janna.

She stares at me with wide curious eyes.

I force a smile. "Go with Aunty Cindy, darling."

"What about my chicken satay and the fried ice cream?" she asks with a frown.

"You'll have that, of course. It's just for a minute so I can talk to this lady here. You don't mind, do you?"

"All right." She slides off the chair obediently and takes the hand Cindy holds out to her. I watch them leave the restaurant before I turn to Star.

"Do you mind if we sit?" she asks.

I sink back into my chair and she sits opposite me.

"Thank you for agreeing to listen to me," she says.

I nod and shrug. "I didn't exactly have a choice."

"No. I'm sorry I ambushed you like this, but I knew there was no other way."

"What do you want, Star?"

She takes a deep breath. "I just wanted to say how very, very, very sorry I am that I didn't trust you."

I stare at her incredulously. "That's it? That's what you want to talk about?"

"It's killing me, Raven. I was unfair to you and I want to apologize. You deserve it. I was so blind, Raven. So incredibly blind. I was so obsessed with Nigel I couldn't see anything else."

I nod. "I see. Now that you have a new man, you've decided your precious Nigel is the liar, not me, and you want to say sorry and make up?"

She looks utterly miserable. "No. It's not like that. I've been on a long journey. I had to learn how stupid I've been."

"He came on to me. I never did anything to hurt you, ever," I cry bitterly.

She winces. "I know that. I have no excuse. I can't even begin to tell you how sorry I am."

"Sorry is just a word, Star. You can't undo the pain I felt when you took his word and didn't even ask me for my version of what happened. You really thought I would try to take the man you loved?"

"I'm here to ask you for your version now."

I shake my head. "It's too late."

She leans forward. "It's never too late. I want to hear the truth from you."

"The truth? What for? All the damage is done."

"Have you never made a mistake before, Raven?"

I sigh.

"Please, tell me the truth. I want to do what I should have done all those years ago. Listened to you."

I make a defeated movement with my hand. "Fine. Remember that night at the barbecue in your house? When Nigel spilled the platter of chicken legs on you and drenched your skirt with sauce?"

She nods. "Yes."

"Rosa and Cindy had already left, but I was still waiting for my dad. You had gone upstairs to change." I take a deep breath. I can see the scene in my mind's eye. Sitting on the patio. The sun had gone down and there was a lovely glow in the sky.

"Nigel had switched on the little fairy lights and they were winking in all the trees at the bottom of the garden. It was so beautiful. I was a bit tipsy so I had curled up in one of the big comfy garden chairs with my glass of wine. I was looking at the lights and thinking how lucky you were, when Nigel said at my side, 'More wine?'"

Star swallows hard.

"None of us were wearing shoes and I had not heard him come up. I looked up at him, a smile ready. Then the smile froze on my face. He was staring at my breasts. His eyes came up to my mouth, then slowly up to my eyes. He smiled and said, 'I love Star, but fuck me, if you're not one sexy bitch. Your lips were made for giving blowjobs. She doesn't need to know. It'll be our secret.'"

Star's eyes widen.

"Yeah, he said that. I was so shocked I didn't know what to do or say. I just stared up at him. I just couldn't say a word. Then he said. 'You've never had a dick in you either, have you?' I swear, I was not encouraging him. I just couldn't react. I was frozen. I almost couldn't believe he was doing that. That was when he reached out and pinched my nipple through my clothes. I woke up from my trance and spilled the wine. And then you came and he held you and kissed you so passionately, I felt as if I was so drunk I had imagined it all."

I take a deep breath. "The next day you came to my house and you just accused me without even asking for my version. I would never, never steal your man, not even if I was stuck alone on a desert island with him for years."

"I'm sorry I didn't trust you. I was such a stupid kid. You looked so guilty when I walked in. And the wine, and the way you couldn't look me in the eye."

I look at Star making excuses for the inexcusable and I don't feel anything. I used to love her. I shrug. "Well, it's all in the past now. Water under the bridge."

"It doesn't have to be. I want us to be friends again. I made a mistake and I want to rectify that. I wish I could explain to you how determined I was to be in love with Nigel. So many people didn't want us to be together. It made me stubborn. I put up with so much shit because I was so determined to make it work. I had a dream so I changed my whole life to fit that dream. I am so sorry. There must be something I can do to make up."

I stare at her. If she offers me money … "What do you want to do to make up?"

"If you need any kind of help, I want you to come to me first. I owe you that."

I shake my head and stand up. "I've got to go."

She stands too. "No, please don't go. I'll go. You stay and have lunch."

"No, I've lost my appetite. You stay." Then I rush to the front door. Outside I can see Rosa and Cindy are each holding one of Janna's hands and swinging her on the sidewalk while she squeals with delight. I open the door and stand there for a moment, confused. Rosa sees me, says something to Cindy, and walks up to me.

"You okay?"

"What do you care?" I snap.

Her head jerks back. "Hey. I'm not the bad guy here."

"No, you're not. You're just the guy who took Star's side without waiting to know the truth."

"Have you ever wondered why I kept in touch with Star and not you?"

I look at her in astonishment. This is just too much. Was she now trying to tell me there was some good reason for her decision? "As a matter of fact, yes, I did wonder. Do tell me why you made that decision?"

"Because Star needed me and you didn't."

"What?"

"You were always the strong one. Star was the one who was in danger from that pedophile. You were so strong and confident you didn't really need anyone. You took on your sister's problems and the responsibility of taking care of Janna. How many of our friends do you think could have done that without batting an eyelid?"

I stare at her.

"Star was not like you. She was vulnerable. Her mum was a selfish bitch who never loved anyone except herself. Even now she only calls Star when she needs money. Star needed me. I couldn't let Nigel win. I couldn't let him alienate her entire support system."

I exhale the breath I was holding. I've done the same thing Star did. I judged Rosa without giving her a chance to explain herself. "I need time to think this out."

She smiles gently. "Okay."

Cindy and Janna appear at our side. "What's the matter, Mummy?"

"Nothing, darling. I've got a headache."

"If you don't want to stay and have lunch we can all go back," Cindy says.

"No, no, you guys stay and have lunch. Janna has been waiting to have her chicken satay and fried ice cream."

"You sure you don't want us to come with you?"

"Absolutely. I'll probably just take a couple of tablets and lie down for a bit. I'll be fine by the time you get back."

CHAPTER SEVENTEEN

RAVEN

I'm happy when Konstantin calls, but unhappy when he says he will be away on a business trip. The next two days pass in a suffocating blur of waiting. By the time Friday rolls around I am in a state of jittery nerves. I wake up early and start making breakfast for all of us. Janna is sitting at the kitchen table, her cheek leaning on the palm of her hand, telling me about a boy in her playschool who keeps using a bad word.

Ever since she found out I would be going away and she would not be coming, she keeps curling herself around me and acting clingy, but Cindy has arranged for her to go see some horses later this afternoon, so even though she is still a bit anxious to be parted from me, she is in a fairly upbeat mood.

"What was the word?" I ask.

"Am I allowed to say it?"

I put a plate of buttered toast strips in front of her. "Just this once."

"Poop."

I put her soft-boiled egg into an eggcup and set it before her. "Hmmm ... That's not very nice of him."

"That's what I said."

I sit in front of her. "Well, here's what I think. I think it doesn't matter what anybody else does. If you think a word is bad just don't use it."

"Mummy?"

"Yes."

"Where is Konstantin taking you?" she asks, nibbling at her strip of toast.

"I don't know. It's meant to be a surprise."

She stops nibbling and looks at me with round curious eyes. "But what if he takes you somewhere you don't like?"

"Well, usually, when someone gives you a surprise they make sure that it's something you're going to like."

She looks concerned. "Is it somewhere very far away?"

"No, darling. Remember, I'm not taking my passport which means I won't even be leaving the country." I smile reassuringly. "I'll be at the end of the phone. You can call me anytime you want."

She nods and dips her finger into the runny yellow of her egg. I hold back from telling her off because I don't want this morning to be anything but happy and fun for her.

"Before you know it, I'll be back. Today you'll go to see the horses, tonight you'll be staying with Nan and Grandad, and tomorrow you'll spend the whole day at Thorpe Park with

Aunty Cindy. You can go on the rides and have candy floss. Would you like that?"

She nods again.

"And I'll be back the next day."

"I'm trying to be brave, but it's really hard," she blurts out suddenly.

My heart contracts painfully. I can't bear to see Janna unhappy. It makes me think I am letting Octavia down. "I don't have to go, little munchkin," I say immediately.

Before she can answer, Cindy's door flies open, and she walks out with chunks of her hair covering her face and her hands outstretched in front of her as if she is a zombie. "Fe Fi Fo Fum I smell the blood of an English girl," she roars in a guttural voice.

Immediately, Janna hops off her chair and shoots across the room. She jumps behind the sofa squealing with fear and delight. Cindy chases her, tackles her to the ground, and starts blowing raspberries on her stomach. She giggles until she is breathless.

It makes me smile to see that Janna has already forgotten to be unhappy because I am going away. I know Cindy will keep her occupied doing fun things while I am gone.

❊

*K*onstantin comes to pick me up in a steel-gray, four door Mercedes. He tosses my small suitcase into its roomy trunk. Dressed in a pair of jeans and a button up shirt he is more casual, but no less devastating. When he turns those hot eyes my way I feel my heartbeat quicken and I remember the fire between us, his hands on me, his lips on mine, and his long, lean body pressing into my own.

He installs me in the passenger side, gets into the driver's seat, and off we go.

"Are you going to tell me where we're going?" I ask.

A small smile plays on his lips as the guarded eyes turn to me. "What is your definition of a surprise?"

"Everything is a mystery with you," I say, only half-joking.

The little smile goes, and his face becomes expressionless. "What do you mean?"

"You never talk about yourself. Ever. I'll admit mysterious men are kinda sexy, but it would be nice to know a little bit more about you."

"What would you like to know?"

"Just give me something. Anything. Even a simple thing about your family."

His expression stays motionless.

"You said you have siblings. How many? Where do they live? What do they do for a living?" I stop myself from going any further. I want to know everything about him, but aiming rapid fire questions at him might be a good way to send him running for cover.

He doesn't take his eyes off the road, or react to my questions, but the temperature drops in the car. A definite chill settles in the air as he answers in a voice completely devoid of emotion. "I had two brothers. They died. Many years ago."

Oh God! Trust me to go and put my big foot into it. Both his brothers died? Must have been some kind of tragedy. Is that why he is so withdrawn and reserved? I knew there must be some terrible things buried deep in his past to explain the don't-come-any-closer air he gives off. I know a little about tragedy myself. I closed off too after Octavia died. Of course, I couldn't turn off completely, not with Janna to take care of.

"I'm so sorry," I whisper. "I didn't mean to bring up something so painful."

The light playfulness of a few minutes ago has completely disappeared, and it's all my fault for prying. Why couldn't I have left good enough alone? Still, can anyone blame me for wanting to know more about a man I'm falling for?

Suddenly he reaches out and squeezes my leg. "No need to apologize. It's hardly your fault. It happened a very long time ago. Let's just enjoy the weekend, okay?"

"Okay," I agree readily.

"What else would you like to know?" he asks.

"Whatever you want to tell me," I say cautiously.

He purses his lips, which I've learned is his way of swallowing a smile. "I've told you everything you need to know. If you feel you need more you'll have to ask me."

I chew at my lower lip. I have a hundred questions, a thousand questions, but now I'm afraid to ask them, afraid that I could unearth more painful events from his past. I don't want to risk stumbling into another landmine.

I go for the safe option. "How old are you?"

"I am thirty-two."

"Okay. Good to know. What kinds of things do you enjoy?"

"What I enjoy? I enjoy fucking you a great deal." His deep voice purrs the words.

"Are you doing that on purpose?" I burst out, cheeks tingling. How easily he can send me sprawling into embarrassment.

He glances at me and smiles. "Doing what?"

"You make me … all hot and bothered. And you do it really well," I say tartly.

He gives a low chuckle. "The feeling is mutual."

"It is? I can't imagine anyone making you feel hot and bothered."

The lights are red and he turns to me, his face dead serious. "You'll be surprised how hot and bothered you make me feel."

I stare at him in astonishment. For a few seconds I can't look away from his face, then he smiles tightly and proceeds to properly answer my original question. "I enjoy good food, fine wines, books, beautiful cars, and … beautiful women."

The last part pierces the soft place around my heart. Just how many beautiful women has he taken away for a weekend? The surge of jealousy surprises me. I've let this go way too fast in such a short amount of time.

My voice is sharp and sarcastic. "Is that what you have listed on your tinder profile? Konstantin, thirty-two, enjoys fine dining, cars, and beautiful women."

He laughs. "I don't have a tinder account."

"This is exactly what I mean. I know next to nothing about you."

"Why the rush, little Raven? You have the whole weekend to get to know me." His eyes slide down to my mouth.

"Yes," I say, breathless for no apparent reason. Sometimes, he just sucks the air out of the room.

"We'll arrive shortly."

We were still in the middle of the city. "I thought we were going away?"

"We are."

Bathed in the luxurious scent of his aftershave, I lean my head back on the headrest and watch the changing view go by my window. I'm not going to ask anything else. It's a surprise. We come to a stop outside an office block.

"Why are we stopping here?" I ask curiously.

"Come on," he says and gets out of the car. He takes the bags out of the trunk and we go into the building. He nods to the receptionist who throws him a dazzling smile. It is not so bright by the time it reaches me.

"Do you work here or something?"

"Nope," he says leading me to the lift.

"This is all very mysterious," I comment.

He grins, but says nothing.

The lift rises to the very top floor, the doors whoosh open and we are on the roof top.

CHAPTER EIGHTEEN

RAVEN

"What the—?" I exclaim, looking at a blue and white helicopter parked on a helipad. I burst out laughing. Surely not. I feel like I am in a movie. "Are we going in that?"

"Yup. I rented it for the weekend."

He throws our bags in and turns to me.

I can't stop smiling. "Where's the pilot?"

"You're looking at him."

I stop smiling. "You're kidding."

"No."

"What? Are you qualified to fly this thing?"

"Sure."

"You are qualified to fly a helicopter."

"Yeah."

I shake my head in surprise.

"It's a very useful skill."

"But this thing has no doors. What if I fall out?"

He smiles. "You won't. You'll be strapped in."

"Really," I say doubtfully.

"Chicken?" he teases.

"Who are you calling chicken?" I ask, and climb in although I'm more than a bit nervous. He straps me in and says with a mocking smile, "Remember you're on vacation so relax and enjoy the ride."

I nod, and he fixes the earphones on me.

Riding in a helicopter is an unexpected experience for me. It isn't like anything I thought it would be. We don't take off violently like in a plane, but practically float up like in a balloon.

I lose all my nervousness almost immediately because of the amazing scenery visible from all sides. It's a strange feeling to be so high up, exposed to the elements, and looking down. Because of the headphones there is no noise and fortunately there is no turbulence either. As we fly over London I thoroughly enjoy myself. Konstantin points out landmarks as we leave the city. The weather is beautiful and the English countryside in summer is just breathtaking.

As we cross Yorkshire county we fly over miles of hauntingly beautiful moorlands. Large swaths of rolling hills are white with flowering cotton-grass and families of beautiful roe-deer graze peacefully below. They seem undisturbed by the sound of the helicopter.

In the distance, I see an austere Gothic castle of gigantic proportions. After the seemingly endless wild beauty of the Moors, the moldering dark-grey stones rise into the air in a melancholic, solitary grandeur of battlements, gateways, towers, and turrets.

"Like it?" Konstantin asks.

"It is magnificent. In a cold, comfortless way."

He laughs. "Think you might like to stay there?"

I feel my eyes grow round. "Is that where we're going?"

He nods.

"Wow! Is it a hotel? It looks so … vacant."

"No. It is privately owned. I rented it for the weekend."

"You mean it will be just us in there?"

"And the ghosts."

My head whirls around. "What?"

He grins. "Most castles in England are haunted. If you're scared you'll just have to stick real close to me, won't you?"

I laugh with a thrill of excitement. The weekend stretches out like a wonderful adventure. I have never stayed in a castle. I'll have to take lots of pictures to show Janna.

Konstantin tells me I don't need to duck to get out of a helicopter, there is no danger of being decapitated, unless of course, the chopper is parked on sloping ground, but out of sheer instinct and watching too many Hollywood movies, I duck anyway.

Close by, an olive-green Lexus is parked. Konstantin fishes a key out of his pocket and lets me in. We drive down the road towards the castle. At ground level, the moors appear inhospitable and desolate. There's not another house in sight. No other cars. Just us.

I lift my eyebrows at Konstantin. "It's very remote, isn't it?"

"The other thing I enjoy is silence."

"But we're kind of in the middle of nowhere, aren't we?"

"That was the idea. I didn't want to share you with the rest of the world." He leans over the center console and trails the back of his fingers on my cheek. It's the first time he's touched me since he briefly squeezed my leg. Soon the barbican comes into view. The five-hundred-year-old grand structure has arrow loops that Konstantin explains were once used to shoot arrows from. He points out the murder hole for dropping projectiles and stones onto the castle's besiegers. As soon as we pass under it we come into the courtyard ringed by a curtain of stone walls. It's like suddenly going back in time. Open-mouthed with wonder I gaze around me.

"Come on. Let's go inside," he says, and gets out of the car. I know how to work the door on this car so I quickly follow him without waiting for him to come around to let me out.

Konstantin grabs our bags from the trunk and we walk up to the castle together. The heavy wooden door is decorated with iron studs that are rusty with age. He pushes it and it swings opens!

"Wow, they left it unlocked."

"This is not London," he says, his palm outstretched to indicate I should enter first. I step into the silent cavern.

Even though the sun shines brightly outside, the temperature is a good few degrees lower in that great hall. Cold vapors coming from the heavy stones touch my skin and make me shiver.

As my eyes grow accustomed to the dim light coming from the high narrow mullioned windows, I make out a vast gloomy rectangular space where the ceiling is so lofty it is at least three stories tall.

The staircase is made of white stone and full of intricate carvings. Numerous low closed doors hint at labyrinths, mysterious rooms or even subterranean dungeons. On one side there is a massive blackened fireplace, and in the center sits a long dining table.

I wonder about the history of the place. The Kings and Queens, the fine noblemen and women who once occupied this castle. They loved and conspired and fought within these grey walls. They are all gone now. The silence is deep and tomb-like. Once we are gone it will return again.

"What do you think?" Konstantin asks. His voice echoes.

I turn to face him. "You could kill me in here and bury me on the moors and no one would know."

He frowns, and a flicker of uncertainty crosses his face. We stare at each other, then his eyes close over. It is as if he is a boy who showed me a secret, special part of his soul, and I mocked it.

"So you don't like it," he says slowly.

I touch his hand, my eyes earnest. "No, I don't like it. I love it." And it is the truth. I love it because this is him. This is the physical manifestation of that chilly, hidden part of him that I cannot reach at any other time.

Electricity suddenly crackles between us.

The craving for him is so strong I want to wrap my legs around him and mount him right there. With a muttered oath he drops the bags and wraps his arms tightly around me. His mouth swoops down on me and his tongue thrusts into my mouth. I grind my hips against him and feel how hard he is. My hands find their way under his shirt, relishing the smooth, muscled contours of his broad back.

Still kissing me, he lifts me off my feet and carries me up the stone staircase toward a pavilion area where faded ancient tapestries cover the walls. There is a huge curtained four-poster bed in one corner. His shoes are loud on the wooden floors. He throws me on the bed and I bounce slightly on the mattress. He takes a condom out of his pocket. Still staring down at me, he unbuckles his jeans and pushes them down his hips.

"Take off your panties and get on all fours," he orders.

It is as if this man has cast a sexual spell over me. I can't say no to him. I pull off my soaked panties.

"Lift your skirt over, push up, lift up your ass, and show me your pretty little pussy. I've been fucking dreaming of it day and night," he says thickly. I hear the tearing of the condom packet as I push my dress up to my waist and expose myself to him. I love the idea that he can't get enough of my pussy. No man has ever made me feel so desirable and wanted.

"Lay your cheek on the bed. Today I'm going to mark you. Everywhere. Your pussy, your mouth, your ass. All of it is going to be mine. You're going to take my cock deep into your body every time you make me hard."

With my ass high in the air, I feel my body open up to him. Wanting that.

"Look at your little cunt. It's fucking throbbing for my cock."

I feel heat climb up my throat at how shameless I have become.

"Raven," he calls throatily.

"Yes,"

"You're going to give everything up to me, aren't you?"

"Yes. Yes, I am. It's all yours."

CHAPTER NINETEEN

KONSTANTIN

*M*y stiff cock is standing straight up and jerking with hunger, and my balls feel heavy with need. The last two days of deliberately starving myself of her have been hell. I roll on the condom and all I can think of is: I want to enter her raw. I reach out and pull her thighs further apart.

I want all of her to be exposed.

She is so pink and wet.

I reach down and lick the honey of her pussy all along the slit. Her sweet smell floods my senses as I push my tongue into her opening. The sensation of my tongue seems to madden her. She calls out my name and writhes with antici-pation. I lift my head and watch more thick, sweet liquid leak out of her. Immediately, I get my tongue on it.

She pushes back eagerly.

It makes me smile to know she wants my cock in her body just as much as I do. I slide my finger slowly inside her, enjoying the heat and tightness. Her pussy sucks my digit in and clenches around it as I withdraw it. I place my slick finger on the ring of her pretty asshole, and she jumps.

"Relax," I say, and smear the puckered skin with her juices.

Not now, but tonight, I'll own her ass too.

The thought almost makes me cum so I grab her hips and thrust into her. She cries out with shock, her hands balling into fists around the sheets, pulling at them helplessly.

"Oh God. You're soooo fucking big," she groans, but she raises her buttocks to get me in deeper. I respond by sinking in balls deep. Her cunt is so fucking tight I've had asses that aren't as taut.

"Play with your pussy for me," I tell her.

I watch her hand slip under my body and her hips jerk with pleasure as her arm moves furiously.

"Harder," she grunts. "Faster."

I fuck her so hard the bedsprings creak. I can tell by her stiffening body that she is about to come.

"Look at me," I command.

She turns her head and her face is already contorted. She can't hold back anymore.

"Go on, cum. Cum on my cock," I command, and she explodes with a scream. As her muscles clench around me, intense pleasure fires down to my cock, and everything else in my body feels numb except for this lightning bolt of pleasure between my legs. I plunge into her one last time hard and let my own release explode inside me.

Even after I return to sanity, her body is still jerking with her own climax. Slowly, her body goes soft, but she doesn't pull away from me.

"I can't move," she pants. "The muscles in my legs feel like they are on fire."

Gently, I push her dress further up and stroke her smooth back. Her waist, her thighs. I bend and kiss her back. The raw electricity is still running between us. With my half-hard dick still buried inside her, I hold her close and kiss her shoulder, the soft curve of her neck.

I never wanted to do this with any other woman. I kiss her cheek, loving the sweet honest smell of her. I want to stay like this forever. I open my eyes. What the fuck am I doing? Why is it different with her? She is like a flower that has somehow managed to sprout on my barren land.

It's just sex. This is just the afterglow. I need to get out of this bed. Like now.

"Are you hungry?" I ask.

She turns to look at me, and damn, if my stomach doesn't twist with need for her. I just had her. She opens that luscious mouth and licks her bottom lip. I swear, she knows the effect she has on me and she's deliberately doing it, because I'm tempted to fuck her all over again.

"I'm starving. I was too keyed up over this trip and leaving Janna to eat more than a slice of buttered toast," she admits, but she looks unwilling to move from the comfort of the bed.

I pull out of her, tie the condom and I spring out of the bed. I pull on my boxers, zip up my jeans, and she curls into a lazy fetal position and smiles dreamily up at me.

The unguarded, trusting smile has a strange effect on me. It makes me feel bad. And sad. Feelings I have not had since ...

"I'll cook lunch for you. Come down when you're ready," I say in my brightest voice, but it sounds fake and shrill.

"What are you going to cook?" she asks, suspecting nothing.

"You'll see when you get your lazy ass down to the kitchen," I throw over my shoulder as I escape from her and the steely tentacles her innocence has started wrapping around my chest.

I can't fall for it. It'll be the death of me.

CHAPTER TWENTY

RAVEN

I stretch and enjoy the luscious afterglow of the orgasm. Until now I have never known that it can actually make one's toes curl. Closing my eyes, I hug the lingering sensation of his fingers running all over my body, leaving a hundred sizzling trails in their wake. I realize my perfect idea for this holiday would involve us never leaving the bedroom. Cindy is right. I've seriously deprived myself.

Now that I have a taste for him, I just want to keep tasting.

After a few moments of staring at the intricate needlework that has gone into the tapestries, I get up and, ignoring my wet thong on the floor, drift down the stone steps. I try to imagine what this castle must have been like in its heyday. The men and the women who must have made this same journey down these stone steps.

My hand trails over the smooth table top. The feasts they must have had here though. Konstantin has left one of the small low doors open so I go in through it. I pass various spaces with low beams and rough walls to get to the kitchen.

It is large and cool. The stone floor is smooth and shiny with use. It boasts a very expensive modern range cooker and an American style double refrigerator. On a thick wooden slab, Konstantin is smashing garlic under the flat of a knife.

I stand at the doorway. "Whatcha making?"

He looks up and grins. "The only thing I know how to. Steak and salad."

"What's the garlic for?"

"My secret ingredient, garlic butter."

I raise my eyebrows, impressed. "Can I help?"

"Nope. Everything is ready."

There is an open bottle of red wine and he nods towards it. "Want a glass?"

"Okay."

He pours the wine into two glasses. I walk into the room and take the glass he holds out to me. He swirls his wine, brings it to his nose and sniffs. I take a sip. The wine is smooth and very fragrant.

"Mmmm. It's really delicious."

"Also potent. That's an Amarone Valpolicella. Sixteen-percent strength," he warns.

Leaning my hip against the table and taking small sips of the heady wine, I watch him work. I can't help but relish the sight of his powerful hands as he chops tomatoes and tosses slices of onions into the salad bowl. I've never had a man cook for me before.

He completes a series of tasks the same way he does everything else—with practiced, precise movements, and in complete silence. It's strange but I no longer have the compulsion to fill the silence with chatter. I feel comfortable and relaxed in his long silences. I feel the wine going straight to my head, making me feel almost woozy.

He shaves parmesan on the salad, then lays the meat on the griddle. It sizzles and spits.

"How do you want your steak done?"

"Medium." He nods and I look around me. "Can I at least lay the table?"

"Already done. We're eating outside."

He turns the meat and looks at me with a smile. "Nearly done."

My heart does a little skip. I don't know why this man has such a startling effect on me. I know something about all this is not right, but I can't stop myself from falling for him. Like a lamb to slaughter I go.

When the steaks are cooked, we carry the food outside to a wooden table just outside the conservatory. The sun shines down on us as we take our seats. The air is so fresh and there is no constant noise of the city here, instead the air is filled with the sound of birds. It feels like we are the only human beings around. There is nothing but rolling, empty land in all directions and open skies.

In my tipsy state, it feels like we have stepped into a painting. If only I could stay in the castle forever with him.

"How's your steak?"

"Tender and juicy," I say, breaking off a piece of baguette and buttering it.

"Good."

I lift a parmesan flake with my fork. "How did you find this place?"

"I once did some work for the man who owns it."

"What exactly do you do for a living?"

"I invest in the city and I fix problems," he says, his gaze set far on the horizon.

I glance up at him, but his light eyes remain occupied elsewhere. Emboldened by the alcohol surging in my veins I try again. "What does that mean?"

He turns to me, his smoldering eyes secretive, his handsome face drawn closed. It's a safe I'll probably never learn the combination to. It takes a few seconds before I realize I'm holding my breath. Even in all this fresh air, it's difficult to breathe when he turns the full intensity of his attention on me.

"You are full of questions today," he notes, his voice much lighter than his expression. "Would you like to go exploring after lunch?"

The look in his eyes tells me he's changing the subject for a reason and that I should just let this go. I'm desperate to know more about him, but I don't want my curiosity to ruin a great weekend.

I take his hand and brush it against my cheek. "I'm not trying to be nosy. I only want to figure you out. You're like a puzzle."

He kisses the top of my head gently. "All mysteries reveal themselves in time." He says each word with care. It's the kind of deliberation that comes with practice, as if he has learned to speak this way. I chalk it up to another part of the mystery, though it niggles at me.

"Do you like it here?" he asks.

I frown at the loveliness around us, the green hills and clear blue sky. "Yes, it's very beautiful."

He shifts and his hand reaches out to me, before he suddenly decides the better of it and changes direction, pointing to the left of me instead. "There is a very lovely spot over that hill. We can have a picnic there tomorrow, if you like?"

I nod, and put the last piece of meat into my mouth. "I'd like that very much. Thank you."

"The pleasure is all mine," he says with a lopsided smile.

"I wish I could have brought Janna. She would have loved it here," I say with a sigh.

He looks at me curiously. "Isn't it too remote for a child?"

I put my knife and fork down and meet his eyes, my lips curving into a smile. "No, Janna is a very special child. She's in love with birds and animals. She won't even let me kill any spiders that stray into the apartment. I have to carefully trap them between a glass and an old birthday card, and set them free on the window ledge. She stands over me to check that I have not broken any of their legs. This would be like a paradise for her."

Something flashes in his eyes, then he blanks it, and glances at his watch. "We should go." He stands and takes me by the hand, and I do what I've done since the night I saw him in that alley—I follow him.

We walk for a long time until we get to an ancient oak tree. The bark is rough against my back as Konstantin stands me up against it and takes me. It is quick and furious. As if neither of us can get enough of each other. Our shouts of ecstasy scare some birds that were nesting in the branches.

Their frantically flapping wings make us laugh.

I realize it is the first time I have seen him laugh properly. I stare at him in astonishment. What a beautiful man he really is. I can hardly believe that such a man would even turn to look at me, let alone fly me away to a secluded castle to have his way with me.

CHAPTER TWENTY-ONE

RAVEN

I have a shower and change into a slinky black dress that Cindy insisted I bring before going downstairs. The temperature drops quickly on the moors and Konstantin has already lit a log fire in the massive fireplace. It warms the room nicely. He must have heard me on the stairs because he comes out of one of the doors and watches me.

He walks up to me. There is something alert and tense about him. "You look beautiful," he says softly.

"Thank you." His eyes make me feel naked and strangely exposed.

"There's only one thing missing."

"What?" I whisper.

He raises his hand and shows me a black butt plug. "This."

My eyebrows rise with surprise.

"Ever used this before?"

I shake my head.

A possessive light comes into his eyes and I feel his need vibrating behind his skin. "No?"

Caught by the smolder in his eyes, I shake my head dumbly.

"Do you want to give up your virgin ass to my cock, little Raven?"

A shiver that steals my breath moves through me. I nod.

"It's gonna hurt some."

I nod again.

"I'm going all the way up, baby. Every last inch is getting buried in there. Are you ready for that?"

The idea that he will be the first to own every part of me excites me. I find my voice. "Yes."

"And once I'm inside I'm going to make you glad you saved that sweet ass for me, because I'm going to fill it up with my cum."

I take a deep breath and his scent fills me. I focus on it. The possessive, dirty talk starts up a fire in my belly. I don't know why, but I want everything he wants. "Yes, I want that."

His eyes blaze. "Good. On the table, spread open on all fours."

He holds out his free hand and I place mine into it. He helps me on the long table and puts me into the right pose. There is a bottle of lube on the table. It is a strange feeling, almost taboo. As if I am the dish that will be consumed. It is both degrading and exciting. I get on my hands and knees on the smooth, hard surface and he takes his position behind me. His hands slip under the slinky dress, his fingers light and warm. Slowly, he slides the dress up and over my hips. I can feel myself become wetter and wetter with excitement.

"Glad to see how excited you are, Raven," he notes.

My insides itch hotly for something I have never had, but I know I want.

Lay your cheek on the table and spread your ass-cheeks apart. I expose myself to him, I feel the change in the atmosphere. He is fighting to control his own urges. The knowledge makes erotic energy course through my whole body.

"Relax and open up," he encourages thickly.

I feel as if I am on fire when he laps up the moisture from my pussy, and uses it to push against the ring of muscles. I hear him reach for the lube and squirt it on his finger. I moan when his slick finger eases in. His finger sinks past the first knuckle. Then the second. Until I feel his hand on my butt cheeks. He pumps his long finger in and out until my inner muscles start throbbing. Then he withdraws his finger, and to my great surprise, I feel the loss of him. He walks over to the front of me and holds the butt plug in front of my lips.

"Wet it," he says.

It slides into my mouth and I suck it. The whole time his eyes rake my face. When he pulls it out a string of saliva hangs from it. He goes behind me and rests the cool lubricated tip against my opening. Leaving it there he rubs my back, shoulders, and neck. Slowly, sensuously. As I moan with pleasure he slips the head in. I tense.

"Relax and push out …" he says softly.

As soon as I do he pushes the plug deeper in. "Just a little bit more," he consoles, when I fret. Then he reaches under me to find my clit and while I groan and twist with pleasure, suddenly, without warning, he jams the plug all the way in.

I gasp.

"There, all done." He pulls my panties over it and comes to the front of me.

"You're now mine to do what I want with. Make sure you know it."

He slaps my ass cheek and I feel the anal plug jerk inside me. Then he guides me down from the table in such a gentle way, that I am more shocked by his solicitous behavior than his claim on my ass.

With the plug inside me we eat stuffed peppers and rabbit stew at the same table where I was stuffed. The food is excellent and we talk as if we are just two strangers who are out on a date enjoying a meal together. He is charming, knowledgeable and interesting, but underneath every word, glance and accidental touch, something primal throbs. I'm entranced by him.

In the firelight his hair gleams like spun gold, and his eyes sparkle as he strokes my hand and asks me if I like the stew.

"I thought you couldn't cook anything other than steak?" I say lightly. Inside I am trembling with fierce need.

"I didn't cook it. It was left in the fridge for us by a woman who lives in one of the nearby villages. I just heated it."

The words are domestic and unremarkable, but our eyes are locked. I can't look away. I forget about the plug and try to cross my legs. Whoa. Bad idea. He smiles knowingly, then leans forward and pushes his tongue into my warm willing mouth. The kiss is long and passionate. I feel devastated by the emotions sweeping through me. He breaks the kiss.

"Who are you?" I whisper.

"Eat. You will need your strength," he mutters.

I continue to eat but taste nothing. We play a game. It is my idea. "As soon as a question is asked you have to say the first word that comes into your head. If you dally there is a forfeit."

"All right. You begin," he says.

"Plum."

He looks amused. "Why?"

I smile back. "Because of the way the word sounds. Plus, I love plums. Now, your favorite word."

"Love."

I stare at him. Amazed. "Really?"

He nods. "Yes."

"Why?"

"Because ..."

"You can't think. You have to say the first thing that comes into your head."

"Because I can't have it."

"Why do you say that?"

He blinks. A strange expression crosses his face. "Do you like your butt plug?" he asks.

I know then I've hit a raw nerve and he has to resort to sex to obfuscate the real issue. "Yes, but only because you put it in there," I reply.

"I want to fuck you with the plug inside you right now."

"Go ahead. I'm here. I'm yours."

He takes me in front of the fire and strips me. Then lays blankets on the floor and gets me on all fours again.

"Are you on the pill?" he asks, his voice a deep rumble.

I turn my head to look at him. "No, but I just had my period."

His jaw clenches. "Then I'm going in raw."

The idea excites me. I want to feel his skin. I want our juices to mix.

CHAPTER TWENTY-TWO

KONSTANTIN

https://www.youtube.com/watch?v=_FrOQC-zEog
(This is not how I am)

*S*he obeys my instruction and lays down on the bed, spreading her legs wide and hooking her knees into her elbows. It hikes her ass up into the air, the plug protruding out of it.

"This is what you want? It's yours and only yours," she offers softly.

I drink in the sight greedily: a beautiful woman spread out before me and presenting her virgin ass for me to plunder. There is vulnerability, complete trust and anticipation in her lovely eyes. As I gaze at her, her eyes widen in surprise at something in mine.

I sit on the bed next to her. Her clit is so swollen the little pearl inside is pushed right out of its hood. I place my lips on the pink bud and suck hard. Incoherent grunts and high-pitched whimpers herald the first spasm that races through her body. I hear her cry out as she braces for a huge orgasm.

On and on her climax goes.

Her clit and pussy convulse, tremble, and clench uncontrollably, and my lips capture it all. Even when the contractions lessen in intensity I keep a gentle sucking motion on the hypersensitive bud. The pleasure is so intense she is nearly sobbing. I see her through the afterglow before I raise my head. I wipe my mouth with the back of my hand and look into her eyes.

She smiles. A secret little smile.

I smile back.

Her pussy is open and engorged, juices are leaking out of it and running down her ass. Picking up the lube, I drizzle it along my thumb. I grasp the head of the butt plug and slowly pull it out of her. She purrs with pleasure as the plug moves inside her.

Her hips jerk and twist when it is out of her. Good. She is missing it.

I lay my thumb on the puckered ring of her ass and she moans and pushes against me to encourage me to enter. Her sphincter is relaxed and my thumb slides into her most private space with hardly any resistance at all. I wait for her second ring to relax fully before I press in.

I raise my eyes to her face and find her watching me. The eroticism of seeing her look at me as I open her ass makes my cock jolt painfully. Gently, I work my thumb past the inner ring, and her ass stretches to accommodate the fleshy base of my thumb.

She rocks her hips and pushes up into me, driving my thumb deeper still until it is buried to the hilt in her gut. She is so excited her pussy runs freely, juices flowing down into my fingers splayed across her ass cheeks. I rotate my thumb and shift my fingers to her pulsing slit.

"Oh God," she exhales, as my fingers play with her clit. It is standing proud from its hood. Like the greedy girl she is, she twists her hips and grinds her clit against my fingers.

I can tell she is on her way to another massive orgasm. I rub her clit and finger fuck her ass until it is too late to halt the orgasm. Then I use my other hand to pinch her clit hard.

She screams and goes completely rigid. As if there is an explosion taking place deep inside her body, her ass clenches around my thumb and her entire body shakes with the powerful force of her climax. For a long time her body trembles and twitches uncontrollably. Possessively, I hold on to her clit. I feel pride to see the effect I have on her body, how I can make it respond so beautifully.

My cock is nearly bursting. "Ready for more?" I ask.

"I'm ready for your cock," she whispers.

She thinks she's ready for my cock, but she isn't. I'll tear her if I enter her now. I lube two fingers and push them into her ass. As soon as the resistance fades, my fingers start to spread the ring of muscles. She gives a lusty moan. Slowly, I ease in and out of her. Every time going a little further.

"You okay?" I ask.

"I love it," she murmurs breathlessly. I begin to rotate with each stroke. Stretching her, readying her for my cock.

"I'm ready now," she says with a touch of frustration.

I pour more lube inside her and make sure my fingers are sliding in easily. Then, I spread lubrication on my cock. The gel is cold, but it is a relief on my burning skin.

"Now I want you to lower yourself onto my cock," I say, sitting with my back against the headboard. She crawls towards me and squats in front of me. Taking my cock in her fist she hovers astride me and positions the tip of my shaft at her back entrance.

Our eyes never leave each other as she slowly lowers her hips. To my surprise, she is so ready and so slick with lube and her own juices I don't feel much resistance as she opens to receive me. As soon as the inner ring adjusts and relaxes, I start travelling into her. Inch by inch her hot, tight velvety passage slides open to take me in. She stops, rises slightly, and sinks back down. With every descent, more and more of me enters her.

"Do I feel good?" she asks.

"Incredible," I reply.

Slowly her ass swallows my cock until her ass cheeks are almost resting on my legs. That is when she does something amazing. Her hands reach back and spreads her cheeks apart. Arching her back she impales herself all the way down until her full weight is on my lap and my cock is all the way inside her. My orgasm has been building, waiting to erupt. I have to fight hard not to blow my load right there and then.

Her juices trickle down and pool between us.

I reach out and touch her swollen pussy. I want to make her climax again while my cock is deep inside her. I make her rut her clit against my hand while she moves up and down my pole. Her breaths come in short gasps.

In seconds she starts to come, her ass clamps my dick, and the pleasure from her clamping ass is so unbearable my whole being suddenly fills with a mindless rapture. I howl out my release as the first blast jets up through my cock, spraying deep into her shuddering bowels. Blast after blast, my balls empty into her.

She sits with her legs open, my cock still buried inside her, and she smiles a tender loving smile. I look at her in astonishment. To open yourself to another and find what you've almost dreamed of.

It's never happened to me before.

Raven

When I rise from his big glistening cock, he asks me to show him my ass. I get on my hands and knees and show him. I don't know what he is looking at, but it makes him laugh darkly.

"What is it?" I ask, turning around.

"Baby, you just gaped for me. Feel it," he says, and guides my finger to my own asshole so I can feel how I have opened up for him.

Then he fucks me again and again, each time my ass willingly opens up to take him in.

CHAPTER TWENTY-THREE

Raven

*W*e come downstairs and Konstantin builds a nest for us in front of the big fire with blankets and pillows. Konstantin covers me with a thick blanket before he goes to stoke the roaring fire. I watch the slabs of his muscles glisten in the light from the flames. I have never seen a man who is so perfectly toned. He must work out like crazy.

He turns his head. "Are you warm enough?"

The air has chilled considerably in the vast hall, but by the fire it is deliciously warm. I nod, feeling satiated and at peace with the world. He gets up and brings the tray of fresh fruit and cheese with our two glasses of wine. He sets them next to me and lays down beside me. I burrow into his hard, warm body. He feeds me cheese, which makes me laugh. He stares at my face and touches my mouth.

"You're so beautiful," he whispers.

I can't keep the dopey smile off my face. Who would have thought that getting attacked and nearly robbed in an alley was the best thing that could have happened to me?

"What are you thinking about?" he asks, his deep voice a gentle purr.

"How lucky I am to have met you that night."

"You did not seem to find it so lucky then. You seemed very annoyed."

I laugh again. "I wasn't annoyed. I was shit-scared. Some guys just attacked me and you showed up out of nowhere like some real-life ninja."

"You were so fiery I was waiting for you to slap my face."

I bite my lower lip. "Slap you? Hell, Konstantin, you have no idea. I was so incredibly attracted to you. Everything about you, your scent, your body, your face, all of it was like a shot of some drug direct into my veins. I was so high I couldn't even think properly." I smile. "And to be perfectly honest, that is still a problem today."

"It's a fucking massive problem over here too. You're so sexy. I can't even concentrate on my work. I just want to fuck you all the time."

I breathe deeply, letting the thrill of that statement wash over me. He's told me I'm sexy a few times now, but I'll never tire of hearing it. The fire crackles loudly and it startles me. He tightens his hold on me.

"I never did thank you properly for that night. I don't know what would have happened if you hadn't arrived when you did."

155

"Yes, it could have been bad for you. Is that the most frightening thing that has ever happened to you?"

I stare hard into the flames, not looking away even as my eyes begin to water. "No," I say after a long while.

"Really? What's worse than being almost robbed and raped?"

The memory drops like a cool weight into my stomach. I close my eyes to say it. I shrug. "It's a tie between two things."

He doesn't speak, just lets me gather my thoughts and decide whether I want to elaborate. I like this about him. His stillness and patience. I'm so used to Cindy, who knows that if she keeps on going I'll eventually break down and tell her whatever she wants to hear just so she'll leave me alone.

I glance up at him. He is looking down at me, but there is that odd, almost sad look in his face. The expression makes me wonder whether I know him at all. I suddenly remember him saying he can't have love. What deep pain does this beautiful man carry in his heart? I decide that it doesn't matter if he won't, or just can't tell me about himself, I'll open up to him. Let him into my pain and my sadness.

"Do you really want to know?"

"Of course," he says immediately.

"The thing that frightened me more than almost being robbed and raped is connected to my sister." I clear my throat. "Janna's mother. Octavia and I were only a year apart, but all my life she had taken care of me as if she was years older. She was very fierce about it. Once she ripped out a fistful of hair from a girl who tried to con me out of my lunch money."

In my mind's eye I see her grabbing the girl, her face

contorted and mean. I squeeze my eyes shut, but the tears are already coming, dripping out from beneath my lids.

"Three years ago she came to see me. I was living with Mum then and I still remember her footsteps coming up the stairs. She sat on my bed and told me she was sick. Breast cancer. But not to worry, they had caught it early. The doctors told her she had a very good chance of beating it. She took my hands in hers and said she was determined to fight it with every fiber she had. She told me all this like we were chatting about the weather."

Not wanting Konstantin to see me cry, I stay curled against his side and wipe my eyes with the back of my hand.

"She was so brave and positive, and there was so much life in her. It is the most unbelievable thing, but I looked at her that day and I knew in my gut that she wasn't going to live much longer. I sat there and pretended everything was going to be all right, but I knew. I knew. I knew. My sister was dying right before my eyes. That was my most terrifying day."

I drop my head further, tears spilling onto my lap. Just talking about that day sends me hurtling backwards and plants me in the middle of the days before Octavia died. Her cool voice crooning to me, and the care she took to comfort me as though I was the one who was dying, and leaving my daughter an orphan.

"I'll never forgive myself for that, for making her comfort me when I should have been the one comforting her." I'm blubbering now. There's no helping it. I can't talk about her, can't even think about her without feeling fragile.

Konstantin takes me into his arms and just holds me while I unravel completely. My shoulders shake as I weep into his chest. His heat is a comfort. I press into it, needing that warmth, that strength. I haven't really let myself lean on anyone since Octavia passed, not even Cindy. I've just kept all of it inside me, locked and hidden. It feels good to let it out, to not hide that burden, even if just for a moment.

When the worst of the tears have passed and I'm less of a sniffling, sobbing mess, Konstantin tilts my face up to his and wipes the last of my tears away. There is a gentle expression on his face that I would never have believed him capable of. His eyes calm me and for the first time I see that he cares for me, honestly and truly. It's such a comfort after so much time alone, struggling to do what I can for Janna.

He kisses my wet face. "Tragedy comes to all of us," he whispers sadly.

A shiver runs down my back, and I nestle deeper into his embrace.

For a while there is only our two hearts beating in perfect harmony. Then he speaks. "And the second thing that frightened you more than three thugs attacking you in that alley?"

I exhale. "I saw a man killed right in front of me."

CHAPTER TWENTY-FOUR

RAVEN

*K*onstantin's body goes rigid. I look up to find him staring at me, his eyes impenetrable as ink. The gentle expression on his face is gone, leaving that façade that I can't get behind.

"When did this happen?" he asks in a low voice.

I whisper my response, as though we might be overheard out here in the middle of nowhere. "It happened six months and nine days ago after my shift. There's a back exit that leads into an alley behind the casino. I used to take it all the time because I can cut over to the next block and catch the bus to my house. The shortcut saves me a good ten minutes of walking around the square late at night."

My heart starts hammering to think of that night. How quiet it was. How frightened and shocked I was.

"I was tired that day and all I wanted to do was get home so I could crawl into bed. I went out of the back exit the way I always did, but that time I heard men talking, which surprised me because I'd never seen anyone back there before. I knew they were speaking Russian since I've heard it at the casino. I can't understand or speak Russian, but something about the urgent way they were going back and forth scared me. So much that I froze. It was dark, they couldn't see me and I couldn't see them."

"So you didn't see them then?" Konstantin interrupts.

"I didn't until they moved. The man with his back to me had a gun pointed at the second man. I think there were other men there, but they did not speak. The man fell to his knees and was begging and pleading but the other man just shot him in cold blood. As he crumpled to the ground, the other man walked up to him, and pumped a few more bullets into him. It was an execution. Then he calmly turned around and walked away with the other men into the night." I shiver again and swallow back the fear rising up from that memory, as well as the image of the dark pool spreading underneath the gunned down man.

"What happened after that?" Konstantin asks.

"I waited until I was sure they were gone then I went back in and told everybody. The police came and interviewed me. The detective in charge, a woman, asked me a lot of questions. After they took the body away," I swallow again, "she took me outside to retrace my steps and show them exactly what happened."

"And you did?"

"Yeah."

"Could you help them?"

"Not really. They wanted me to identify the man with the gun and I couldn't."

"You didn't see the man's face then?"

I nod a single time. "Yes, I did. Once he killed the other man, he turned slightly and the light from one of the streetlamps shone on his face and I saw him perfectly. I looked through hundreds of mugshots but he was not in any of the photos they showed me. I still see his face in my dreams sometimes. I know I could identify him if I ever saw him on the street. I looked for him everywhere for weeks, always expecting him around every corner."

Konstantin draws me to him, holding me more tightly than before. I can hear his heart thudding in his chest. "Oh, my poor little Raven," he whispers in a voice that is choked with emotion. Is he upset?

"You're the first person I've told besides the police and Cindy."

He doesn't answer, just holds me more tightly with one arm while his other hand slides up my skirt and between my legs. I draw in a sharp, surprised breath, but I don't fight him when he pushes me onto my back.

He climbs on top of me, lips finding my neck and hands shoving my legs open. He pushes inside me, his hard cock like a spear. His shoulder muffles my gasp of pleasure.

The sex is entirely different this time, his strokes rough and urgent. The way he crushes his hot mouth to mine seems wildly desperate. Grunting and breathless we climax in a frenzy of pleasure and pain. He collapses on top of me with his full weight, flattening me on the blankets, his heart racing against my chest, both of us panting, our exhausted limbs tangled and useless. Still breathing heavily, he slides most of the way off me, keeping me pinned down beneath the leg and arm he leaves draped over my body.

I turn my head to the side to find him staring at me. The light's so dim, I can't see his eyes clearly, but what I can see of his face is so serious.

"You could have died that night," he whispers.

The day is catching up to me—the drive, the sex, the constant vigilance that seems to be the cost of being around him, like the mystery of him takes a physical toll.

I kiss the tip of his nose. "Did my story upset you?"

He stares at me for another long moment before answering. "Yes, Raven. Your story upset me a lot."

I wish I could see his eyes more clearly. It's the only part of him that doesn't seem capable of locking up. They are the only way into that impenetrable façade.

"We live in a horrible world," he mutters. The fire crackles. I touch his face, tracing his strong jawline so I can feel the muscle clenched there.

"Are you referring to your brothers?" I whisper.

His eyes never waver. "Yes."

I scoot into him. "Do you want to talk about it?"

"Talking does nothing," he says emotionlessly.

"It helped to talk to you about my sister."

"My entire family was taken in a single day," Konstantin says in a strange voice. Again the flat, colorless, tone of voice, the lack of inflection. Is this loss why he is the way he is? So chilly and detached?

I hold my breath, waiting for him to continue.

He says nothing.

"You have me," I say.

He holds me more tightly. "Have I?"

"Yes. You have me, Konstantin." I press my face into his chest, inhaling the rich, masculine smell of him. The drowsiness overtakes me slowly. I close my eyes, surrendering, and tumble headlong into dreams of dark alleys and gunfire.

❋

I wake in the dark, disoriented, my heart racing from a dream I can't really remember. After a moment, I recall where I am. In a castle on the moors. With Konstantin. I turn to search for him, but I'm alone. I sit up slowly, looking around. I'm in the living room in a warm cocoon of blankets and pillows before a dying fire. The orange embers are cooling slowly.

I sit and look around. I see him immediately.

He is sitting naked and cross-legged on the table. Moonlight from one of the tall windows falls on his blond hair making it glint. His shoulders are hunched, but his handsome face is illuminated by the moonlight pouring in from one of the high windows so I can perfectly see his expression.

I want to go to him, but I can't.

I am stunned by the sorrow that surrounds him. It is so huge it fills the entire hall. This is the first time I've seen him without his guard up, without that charming façade he wears. My heart starts to hurt for him. *Oh, Konstantin. What is it that troubles you so? Tell me. Let me in. Let me do something for you. Let me help you. I love you.*

A part of me could watch him all night like this, savoring the unfamiliar sight of him so unguarded and open, but I want to comfort him if I can. I rise slowly from the blankets, not wanting to disturb him. Naked I cross the room soundlessly.

He feels my presence a few seconds before I reach him, and turns away, hiding his face from me. I lean into his back, pressing my cheek against his frozen skin. With a deep sigh, I wrap my arms around him.

"I love you, Konstantin. I know it is too soon to say it. I know it could push you away for good, but it's the truth and I want you to know it."

For a brief second, he tenses, his muscles solid as a rock, and then he relaxes into my embrace. The relief is palpable.

Someone loves him.

Someone loves him.

CHAPTER TWENTY-FIVE

KONSTANTIN

(Twenty-seven years ago)
https://www.youtube.com/watch?v=SF0mG2TtGvw
(I forgive you)

I live with my family in a house made from mud and
hay. It is very small, but it has everything we need in it.
There is a kettle sitting on a black stove, there are cups and saucers
on the shelves. There is always wood for the fireplace in winter, and
there is laughter all year round.

*My mother is sitting at the table preparing food for us. Grandad is
half-asleep in front of the television. An old black and white movie
is playing. We have no electricity, but my father has hooked a live
wire to the grid and we steal all our power from there. It is a
dangerous affair so I am not allowed to go near it. My two brothers
are out working on the land with Papa.*

When I grow up I will work the land too.

My grandmother is in the shed collecting eggs and cleaning out the chicken coop. We keep our chicks in wooden crates. They are lovely and warm to hold, but I no longer have permission to go near them. Ever since I accidentally squeezed one of the chicks so hard it suffocated and died I have been banned from going into the dimness of the shed.

I am very sad about it because I know my father was furious with me. He thought I was being senselessly cruel to a helpless animal, and he lost his temper, shouted at me, and told me he was ashamed of my behavior. A real man doesn't hurt a helpless creature. Only a coward does that.

I tried to explain, but he didn't want to hear. He left the house with a scowl, but my mother understood. She knew Mishka was my favorite chick, that I loved her, and I was only trying to love her better. Instead of cooking Mishka, she let me give her a burial at the back of the house. I cried when my mother shoveled dirt over her still, lifeless body.

With carelessness, I had killed the thing I loved dearly.

"Mama, where has Mishka gone?"

"Mishka has gone where all innocent creatures go. To heaven," she said.

"What's heaven like?" I sniffed, curious.

"Well, since she was a chicken, heaven is large pasture. There are no cages there. No one will steal her eggs. All the feeding troughs are full of seeds and the ground is full of juicy worms. There are no foxes so she can even stay out all night to look at the moon if she so desires."

I frowned. "But, Mama. What about the worms then? Do they have to get eaten even in heaven?"

For a moment, Mama was stumped then she said, "Only bad worms go to the chicken heaven so they can be forever eaten. Good worms go to the heaven for where there are no chickens to eat them and they can live happily in the rich soil and the sunshine."

That made me happy. To think that we lived in a fair universe. Do good and you are rewarded. Do bad and get bad in return.

"Do good people go to good people heaven when they die too?"

"Yes, my little bear."

"Will you go to heaven, Mama?"

She grinned. "I hope so."

"What's heaven like for good people?"

"Well, it says in the holy book that heaven is the most beautiful garden you could possibly imagine. Full of greenery, cool shade, and running water. There are orchards full of fruit trees, fields of fragrant flowers, and angels come to greet you when you arrive at the gates. No one has to work. There is much to eat. Everybody is always happy and there is no such thing as sorrow."

I listened to my mother in awe. "Will our whole family go there?"

"If we are all good, I don't see why not?"

"But ... what about Mishka? I killed her."

My mother took my hand. "That was an accident, little bear. You will not be judged for that. Mishka knows you loved her and so does God."

I frowned. "Is it Papa's God or yours that knows?"

"Papa's God and mine are the same. Just like you call me Mama and papa calls me darling and grandma calls me Nura."

Did I tell you that my father is a Serbian and my mother is a Bosn-

167

ian? My father is a Christian and my mother is a Muslim, but that did not stop them from loving one another. They loved each other with a passion that often made my grandmother ask for a sick bucket to be brought to her.

Later that day I laid a purple flower on Mishka's grave, and went about my business. I had to pick firewood, climb trees, slide down the mudbank with my friends, cycling for miles, catch rats ... life was good, you see.

It was better than heaven for good people.

CHAPTER TWENTY-SIX

RAVEN

"*W*hat's wrong?" I whisper, not wanting to ruin the magic of this night. The delicate spell cast by the dying fire and the extraordinary sight of this powerful man sitting naked in the moonlight.

He turns his face slowly and I prepare myself for that forlorn boy I glimpsed from the blankets just a few moments ago. I prepare my face, putting on a gentle, loving expression, not wanting to discourage him from being open with me, but already that lost child has been replaced by the mask.

By the man who smiles as his eyes burn holes right through me. The one who can turn chilly in an instant, freezing out whoever is around him. The sudden change in him leaves me wordless and sad to my core. Will it always be like this? Will he trust me enough one day to open up? Will I have the strength to wait that long?

I don't speak as my stony-faced enigma, my back-alley James Bond, sprints nimbly to the ground. He lifts me off the ground and carries me back to our nest by the fire. He sets me down on my feet and presses his hungry mouth onto mine. All the questions I have for him dissipate in the strength of his desire, my legs going soft so it's easy to sink onto the ground again when he does, our limbs tangling and kisses growing more desperate, as we fuse together. The coupling is quick and furious.

He looks into my eyes, his face flushed and tight as he plunges into me one last time. He roars my name as he shoots into me, pulse after pulse of hot seed, filling me.

*T*he weekend passes in a blur of passion. We forgo just about every activity in favor of sex in the bedroom, the nest of blankets by the fire, the two-seater dining room table, the bathroom with the throne like toilet, and outside on the grass beneath a sky full of twinkling stars. We are like two kids who just discovered the magic of mating.

We forgo the picnic by the water, the scenic drive through the country, the walks along the grounds. The only break we take from the desperate lovemaking comes in the form of meals Konstantin prepares, his skill in the kitchen demonstrated by a variety of delicious dishes he concocts without the assistance of a cookbook or access to Pinterest.

By the time we leave, locking the door to the castle behind us and tossing our things into the trunk of the car, it is early afternoon. As we are about to get into the car I turn back to look at the castle where I have spent the most exciting and wonderful two days of my life, and I feel an unexplainable sense of foreboding.

As if something bad is waiting for me outside these gray

courtyard walls. A sensation of loss. A feeling that I'm leaving something behind. Whatever Konstantin and I shared here is gone forever. The vulnerable, tender man I found within the castle doesn't live in the outside world.

"You sure you got everything?" Konstantin asks. The wind blows at his hair, lifting and dropping it on his forehead. I love his hair. It is so silky and thick I could run my fingers through it all day long, but he pushes it back impatiently.

I shrug. "I could have missed a piece of soggy underwear in some corner, otherwise I'm good."

"No doubt the maids are used to finding worse," he says dryly.

My heart hurts suddenly. He is a man of the world, perhaps for him our time here was just a dirty weekend. I force a smile and get into the car.

The reception at the castle was terrible and I only spoke to Janna once. I know I shouldn't, but I feel a bit guilty that I was enjoying myself while I was away from her. I send a text to Cindy.

Getting on the road. Tell Janna I'll see her soon!

Her reply is impressively fast.

Janna doing happy dance. Text us 15 minutes before you arrive.

A smile tugs at my lips. I can imagine her prancing around like that dancing little girl from her favorite YouTube video.

Tell her I can't wait to see her.

Her reply is tongue in cheek.

WHAT ABOUT ME????

I smile. I have a nice life. If only I could have Konstantin it would be perfect.

You too. Can't wait to see you!

The journey is mostly accomplished in silence, as if he too feels the same sense of loss that is settling around my heart. I send another text to Cindy when I am fifteen minutes away so I'm not at all surprised to find both of them waiting outside our apartment building. Cindy grins at me and waves, but as soon as Janna spots us she starts jumping up and down like a rubber ball. Pulling at Cindy's hand she makes her run out to the street to meet us.

"Hang on, hang on," I shout as Konstantin pulls up to the kerb. I leap out of the car, drop to my knees and throw my arms open. A squealing Janna launches herself directly into them. The feeling of her little body warms my sad heart.

"I missed you, munchkin!" I say, hugging her tightly.

Her hair tickles my cheek as she starts wriggling because she wants to speak. I end the hug and she twists away from me. Beaming her sweetest smile, the one that brings out both her dimples she says, "Cindy and me had loads of fun!"

"Cindy and I," I correct.

She completely ignores the grammar advice and rattles on about the ponies she has seen. One was just born and only a few inches taller than her, she says, her hands gesturing and her eyes round with wonder.

I know where she is going with this.

"He could so easily live with us, Mummy."

Konstantin comes around the car to stand next to me. Without warning, Janna jumps up and seizes his long legs in a hug, her head barely reaching past his thighs.

I smile up at Konstantin to apologize for her irrepressible-puppy-like behavior, but he's looking down at her and smiling tenderly. He caresses her dark curls with his hand and the gentle sweetness of the gesture squeezes my heart. It hits me in that instant that I'm not just in love with this man. That ship has long sailed. I'm utterly, completely and totally besotted with him.

He turns to me and suddenly that genuine, unscripted warmth chills. His eyes change.

"I will be away on a business trip for the next several days."

"Where are you going?" I ask, surprised by the existence of this sudden, mysterious business trip that didn't come up once over the last forty-eight hours.

"Nowhere interesting," he says with a polite smile, but his expression is tight and closed.

"I did a painting. Do you want to come in and see it?" Janna asks tugging at his hand.

Konstantin tears his gaze away from mine and looks down at her. "I'm afraid I'm late. Another day, okay?"

"Okay," she says and skips over to me.

In all the confusion and Janna's excitement, it is not possible to say goodbye to Konstantin properly. He pulls my bag out of the trunk and Cindy takes it from him. Janna holds her hands up to me and I lift her up. With her clinging to my neck I turn to him. He goes around the car to the driver's side and stands looking at me. For a second he looks lost.

In that moment, his eyes burn with a strange light, and he seems on the brink of telling me something important. I hold my breath with anticipation. Then he shakes his head and gives me one of his charming smiles. I've already learned how fake they are.

"Well, I'll see you then," he says, and moves to climb into his car.

"Konstantin," I call, putting the wriggling and super-hyper Janna down.

"Yeah?"

"Thank you for the weekend. I had an amazing time."

"No problem."

I know it sounds desperate, but I can't help myself. "When will I see you again?" Now Janna is hanging on my legs, hugging as hard as she can and giggling into my thighs. I lean to put my hands on her tiny shoulders and give them a squeeze.

"I'll call you." Then he gets in, and motors away, leaving the three of us on the sidewalk.

"*W*hat was that all about?" Cindy asks as we go in through the front door.

"I don't know," I admit.

"Show Mummy the photos of the ponies," Janna demands.

Cindy dutifully takes her cellphone out of her purse, finds the pictures of Janna and the ponies and hands it over to me.

I take it from her and swipe through them with Janna hanging to the side of the sofa and giving me a running commentary. I nod, smile and make the appropriate noises, but my mind is whirling.

Finally, I look into Janna's face. "Can you go watch Frozen for fifteen minutes while I talk to Aunty Cindy, darling?"

"But that's not fair," she grumbles, flinging her hands down in protest. "I never get to spend time with you."

"Look what I've got for you," Cindy says, holding up a Twix bar. She trundles off quite happily after being bribed with a finger of chocolate.

"So tell me," Cindy says settling next to me.

As I open my mouth to talk to her about Konstantin, Janna comes back in. Determined to spend more time with me she has stuffed the Twix bar into her mouth as quickly as she can. Still chewing, she climbs into my lap. I decide that everything else can wait. I'll give her the time she needs. Soon she'll be wanting to hang out with her cool friends and I'll be begging her to spend time with me. I kiss the top of her head and listen to all her stories until it is dinnertime.

That night she even wants to sleep in my bed.

Even though I give her my whole attention, a little part of me is alert and waiting for the sound of a message coming through on my phone.

It never comes.

CHAPTER TWENTY-SEVEN

RAVEN

*A*fter breakfast Janna goes to her room and busies herself with choosing her outfit for the day. I can hear her singing *Twinkle Twinkle Little Star*. It's usually quite a long process since she has very definite ideas about what she wants to wear. Quickly, I take my phone and type in a message for Konstantin.

I had such a really great time with you. Thank you. Can't wait to see you again.

I consider erasing the last part. Maybe it makes me sound too desperate. I don't even know what would be the cool thing to say after a weekend away. I don't want to come across as clingy. At the same time I want to be real. In the end I leave it in. I want him to know how I feel about him. I want to see him again, desperately.

After I click Send remorse sets in.

It's been so long since I dated anyone. What if I've just sent him running in the opposite direction? I didn't hear from him last night, which, if I am honest, surprised me. After our incredible weekend together the least he could have done was send a little goodnight text. Even so, I didn't want to crowd him, so I purposely waited until this morning.

Cindy's advice would help, but she's at her mom's place.

I scowl at my phone until Janna appears at the doorway in her blue Frozen costume, sparkly tiara, pink socks and a pair of yellow sandals.

"Does my bum look big in this?" she asks.

"What?" I ask with a surprised laugh.

"Does my bum look big in this?" she repeats, turning to give me a view of her small bum.

"No, it doesn't. It looks very cute, as a matter of fact."

"You will tell me if it does," she says, coming into the room.

"Of course," I say with a laugh.

"Okay," she says happily.

"Where did you hear the thing about the bum?"

"Marie asked Aunty Cindy while we were out shopping."

Marie is one of Cindy's friends. "I see."

"What are we doing today?"

"Well, since we did a lot of going out last week, I thought we could stay in for a change and do some flashcards and reading."

She pushes her bottom lip out. "Do we have to?"

"Yes, we do, but while I'm doing the laundry and the ironing you can do some painting. Maybe you can paint some ponies. How bout dat, huh?"

She grins and nods eagerly.

✳

*J*anna and I spend an hour with her sight word flashcards. Afterwards, while I get on with the laundry, cleaning, and ironing, she creates three masterpieces with her fingers. Leaving them to dry on the kitchen table I run the bath for her.

By the time she is washed and dressed, Konstantin still hasn't responded to my message. I stare at my phone willing a reply from him to magically appear in my inbox.

Disappointed and sad, I finish getting ready for work, drop Janna off at Bertha's and take the tube to the casino.

✳

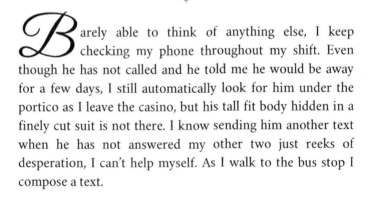

*B*arely able to think of anything else, I keep checking my phone throughout my shift. Even though he has not called and he told me he would be away for a few days, I still automatically look for him under the portico as I leave the casino, but his tall fit body hidden in a finely cut suit is not there. I know sending him another text when he has not answered my other two just reeks of desperation, I can't help myself. As I walk to the bus stop I compose a text.

How's your trip going so far? I just had a great night at work.

I frown. That looks too boring. I add another couple of lines.

How's your trip going so far? I just had a great night at work.
Well, not exactly great, but not terrible either. Tell me
about you.

*B*efore I can change my mind I send it.

I arrive home without a reply to any of my messages. After collecting Janna, I change out of my clothes, splash cool water on my face, brush my teeth, and slip into bed, but I can't sleep.

I'm physically exhausted from the long day, but my thoughts won't calm down. The heat between us. The sizzling jolts of electricity every time we touched. The hungry, desperate way he made love to me after I found him on the table. None of it makes sense in the light of this sudden, unexplained silence. I keep seeing him, looking utterly lost in the light filtering in through the window.

I sit up suddenly and hug my knees, certain that something is terribly wrong. What if something has happened to him to make it impossible for him to send me a reply? He could be hurt. Or dead.

I shove my mind away from the last possibility, which is obviously a ridiculous, hysterical thought. He's probably just out of cell range. Another part of my brain chimes in: or a jerk.

I pace my bedroom floor.

Of course, it's entirely possible that he got exactly what he wanted from me—a weekend of no strings attached sex—and has now gone on his merry way. Guys like a conquest, right?

The idea doesn't infuriate me to righteous anger the way it should. It sinks me into a deep, miserable hole. I really like this guy. Janna likes him. If he disappears on us, I'll be heartbroken.

CHAPTER TWENTY-EIGHT

RAVEN

https://www.youtube.com/watch?v=9Pes54J8PVw
Simply falling

I sleep badly and wake up to a silent, empty phone.

I pretend to be bright and happy in front of Janna, but after I take her to Tuesday preschool, I return to the apartment in a confused, dazed state. Did I imagine the connection between us? Is he just a very efficient player after all? Another part of me jumps in, absolutely refusing to believe it. Nobody can pretend like that. What we had was real.

I switch on the TV and flick through the channels without any interest.

I yawn and it occurs to me I'm tired. Maybe I should sleep for a bit. I stand in front of the door to my bedroom and know there is no use going in, I will never be able to relax. I am too tense and unhappy.

I need to talk to Cindy, but she is still asleep.

I walk to the kitchen and take out a carton of ice cream from the freezer. I put three scoops into a bowl and suddenly tears start running down my face. I sink into a chair and stare unseeing out of the window.

"Don't cry, Raven. You'll be all right. Everything will be all right," I whisper fiercely.

I cover my eyes with my palms and take deep calming breaths. *Don't cry.* No, I won't cry. I fell too fast and too hard. I'm not being rational. He could have a perfectly good reason. He must do.

Maybe his phone has been stolen or lost abroad. Or he could be sick. Something could have happened. I shouldn't jump to the worst conclusions so quickly. I cling to that comforting belief even though in my heart, I know his phone is not lost or stolen, and nothing has happened to him that will stop him from picking up his phone and answering me.

"Hey," Cindy calls from the doorway.

My palms fall away from my eyes and I turn to her. She is still wearing her pajamas and her hair is tousled. She takes in my unhappy face in one glance, but she keeps her voice steady and practical. I love that about her. Everything is solvable. No drama is worth it.

"Are you eating ice cream at this time of the morning?"

"He hasn't called," I say, diving right in.

Her eyes widen slightly. "No?"

"Not even one lousy text since he dropped me off."

Her chest rises and falls in a sigh. "Want to tell me what happened?"

I nod, feeling bad that I am throwing all this at her before she even has a chance to wake up properly.

"Let me just get some coffee first. You know what happens when I don't get my caffeine fix in the morning," she says heading towards the kettle.

I jump up. "No, you sit down. Let me make it." It will be better for me to do something with my hands. I make a mug of coffee, place it in front of her, and take the seat across from her. She curls her hands around the hot mug, takes a sip, and looks at me.

"Okay, hit me with the worst."

I tell her about the weekend, the great sex, and that deep connection I felt existed between us, but I don't tell her about finding him staring up at the moon through the window that night. Seeing a man who so protects his privacy that unguarded and vulnerable still feels like an intrusion. Telling someone else would feel like I was completely breaking his trust. Not that he actually confided in me or anything like that, but even taking me to the castle was his way of showing me a part of himself.

"I don't understand what could be wrong, Cin. I miss him so much and I can't bear the thought that this could be the end. What if he never calls me back or I never see him again?"

"Aren't you being too dramatic? He hasn't disappeared into the ether. He did tell you he was going away on a business trip."

I widen my eyes in surprise. "Since when does going on a trip mean you can't give a girl a call, or reply to her text messages?"

She lifts her palms in a conciliatory gesture. "You're right. I agree with you that he should have called and replied to your texts, but before you get on your high horse you have to see the big picture."

"What big picture?" I demand. "I know for a fact that if any man did that to you, you'd cross him off your list for good."

"Yes, but I've never gone out with a man like Konstantin."

"What do you mean?"

"He's different. There's something deep about him. He didn't come across as a wham, bam, thank you, ma'am kind of player. I can't believe he's had enough. That look he gave you when he dropped you off was, I'll admit, complicated, but it was also so full of raw emotion it made my hairs stand on end."

"Really?" I ask, clutching at the straw that someone else witnessed the connection I was beginning to think I had imagined.

She nods slowly. "Absolutely. You're almost certainly right that something is wrong, but it's not because he doesn't want you anymore. Maybe he has a legitimate reason for not getting back to you. Or perhaps he has issues. You know, commitment stuff."

I think of how I told him I loved him. Oh, what a prize jackass I've been. Fool. Fool. Fool. He was telling me in so many ways that he needed space and time, but I just ignored all of it, blundered in with talk of love. I've probably scared the living daylights out of him. The tears start burning the backs of my eyes, which pisses me off.

This is exactly why I didn't want to date anyone. It complicates everything. I dash away the tears roughly. "I'm not cut out for this bullshit, Cin. Really, I'm not. Maybe I just need to go back to focusing on Janna. I was happy when it was just the two of us."

"Oh, Raven. Never dating again isn't the answer."

I stare at her gentle eyes. "If I can't have him I don't want anybody else. I know I won't find what I had with him with anyone else. I know that without a shadow of a doubt, Cin."

"Look. You're already in this. Why not just wait for a few more days and see what happens? As far as I'm concerned this show isn't over. I haven't written him off yet. Not by a long shot, but even if we take the worst-case scenario and he turns out to be a complete jerk, he made you happy for a little while. He got you to go somewhere besides the park and the casino. That's a good thing, Raven."

"Is it really?" I ask bitterly.

"You had fun, didn't you?"

I shrug, feeing heartbroken. "Yes, I had fun, but I didn't go into this for fun. I never wanted a casual fling with some random guy. I felt something with him. Something real. From the first day there was something there. I thought I was getting that vibe from him too. I even let him meet Janna. That's how much I felt for him."

Cindy sighs wearily. "Maybe he felt all the same lovey-dovey stuff for you too, and it scared him. Guys are like that. If things move too quickly, they put the brakes on and don't really think about how deeply it affects the woman in the meantime."

I try to process what she just said. When it comes to dating, Cindy is a bit of an expert. All the men she dates fall hard for her and she is the one who always breaks it off. Her mantra is: the more you love them the less they love you so she never gets very emotionally attached to any of the men she dates.

"Actually, isn't that exactly what you do to the men you date?" I ask, and attempt a weak titter, but it fails miserably. I'm too fragile right now.

"Yeah, I guess it is," she admits.

"I don't know what to do. Should I give him his space? Keep messaging him? Ignore him if he finally does contact me?"

"Depends on how much you like him." She pauses. "And how petty you want to be."

"What would you do in this situation?"

"I don't know how I'd react with a guy like him, but I'd trust that he wasn't calling because of something deep and complicated. I'd definitely give him a bit of time, but I'd have a cut-off point in my head. A piece of rope. He can go so far, then I'm yanking it away and that would be the end of us and him."

I think on this a moment. "If he doesn't answer … that would mean all he wanted was sex."

"Not necessarily. That reasoning is too simple for a guy like that. I would be thinking up more complicated scenarios."

"Like what?"

"I don't want to speculate. Let's wait and see, huh?"

I look at her curiously. "You're supposed to be cheering me up,"

She smiles. "I'm getting there. Just taking the scenic route."

"It's not very scenic from where I am sitting," I grumble.

"Just think. A man like that. With his looks and money, does he really need to chase any woman? They must be fainting at his feet all the time. Be patient. Give him the benefit of the doubt. You went with your gut and put all your cards on the table. Let's see what he comes back with."

She's right. I'll give him a chance. Konstantin and I had a connection, which is why this hurts so much. I want to spend as much time with him as I can and I don't understand why he won't.

"How long would you wait for him?" I ask, my voice squeezed tight with the sobs building in my chest. I don't want to cry over him. After Octavia died, I thought I'd never stop being sad, but even that overwhelming sadness came to an end. If I never see Konstantin again, I know I'll get over it eventually, but the spark of hope for the future that he kindled in me will die with him.

"Give him at least a day or two, Raven. Let him work through whatever stuff is going on with him. If he's dumb enough to let you go, then he doesn't deserve to be in your life anyway."

I drop my head. Nothing she's said has comforted me. The fear that I will never see him again is too immense. The idea devastates me. I cannot explain it to her. For all her experience she has never been in love. "Thanks, Cindy," I say. My voice is hoarse from holding back the tears.

"Dating is hard," she says softly, "but if you really like this guy then at least give him the time to realize he hit the damn jackpot when he jumped in to save your ass that night in the alleyway."

My lips tremble into a smile. "I guess he did save me."

"I think that earns him a little leeway, doesn't it?"

"Yeah," I mumble.

"And … just for the record, you've seen him without his clothes and that's something. I'd pay good money to see that guy naked." She makes an appreciative noise.

I hack out a laugh. Mum always said don't go around spreading your misery. She's tried her best to comfort me and failed, so I'll just suck it up and pretend. "Sorry, Cindy. I love you, but I'm not sharing."

"Bitch!" she says with a smile, but the smile doesn't quite reach her eyes.

I guess I haven't fooled her and she hasn't fooled me.

CHAPTER TWENTY-NINE

RAVEN

https://www.youtube.com/watch?v=euCqAq6BRa4
(Let Me Love You)

*I*t's Thursday night and my shift is over. I haven't slept well the last few nights. Lots of nightmares and lying awake staring up at the ceiling. I wake up with my shoulders tense and sore, as if I've been lifting weights in my sleep.

I sent Konstantin one final message yesterday afternoon before my shift. I was dying to rant at him about how hurt I was by his silence and to tell him to go to hell for treating me so dismissively, but I realized that Cindy is right. I'm crazy about him so I owe it to myself to give him a bit more time. If there was even a tiny hope that I could see him again, I'll take it. After agonizing about it for nearly an hour I came up with a message that was pretty upbeat, I thought.

You're probably very busy. Maybe message or call me when you're back in town? x

Of course, there was no reply.

After my shift I walk through the casino's massive entrance doors, dragging my feet. Sometime about ten tonight I picked up a tension headache and my head is throbbing like a drum.

Thinking about splurging on a taxi tonight I look to the left where they are parked and to my shock I see Konstantin is waiting for me.

He's leaning against the Mercedes he used when he came to pick me up for the weekend. Our eyes lock and I freeze. Stock still, we stare at each other. He's dressed more casually tonight in a button up shirt tucked into a pair of dark trousers. He's had a haircut too, which kind of hurts me, because it makes him even more unapproachable and foreign.

I inhale sharply when he straightens and starts striding towards me.

God, the man knows how to walk! Less than a foot away he stops. Instantly, I breathe in his cologne and it makes me almost swoon. I try not to show how excited I am to see him. Instead I call on the anger and hurt that I felt over the last few days when he couldn't even be bothered to pick up the phone to call or text me. I let how small and unwanted that made me feel simmer in my gut.

Plus, he took the time to get a haircut! Bastard! The time I spent worrying and crying. Just thinking of the tears I shed pisses me off so much I want to slap him right there on the street.

His face is as impenetrable as a brick wall. I know there are feelings back there somewhere. I've seen them, but, right now, he's giving me nothing. We could be strangers for all the emotion he shows.

"You don't look well," he says, his hand reaching up to my face.

I jerk away from his touch. "Concerned, are you? Why didn't you answer my messages? What the hell are you doing here?" I ask through gritted teeth. The air between us throbs with resentment and anger.

"Will you come to my apartment?" he asks.

My cheeks ignite, my entire face flushes. "Are you serious?" I gasp.

He has the gall to nod.

So much for pretending none of this bothered me. "We haven't even spoken in days. You could have been dead for all I knew and yet, here you are wanting me to jump right back into bed with you? What do you think I am? A whore?" I seethe.

His head jerks back. "It's not for that. I need to talk to you. I had to go away … to make a few decisions."

My hands find their way to my hips. "So, it wasn't a business trip?"

"Not quite," he concedes.

"You lied?"

His posture becomes suddenly tense, giving me the impression of something coiled and ready to attack. His eyes are different too, wary and uneasy.

"I will tell you why I left, but it cannot be here. It must be in private."

The tension in his voice and body penetrates my defenses. I recognize the urgency in his gaze. My anger disappears and adrenalin and instinct rush through my body. All my senses kick into high alert. He doesn't want to bed me. He's afraid. Something is about to happen. Something terrible.

"What's wrong?" I ask, my voice a frightened whisper.

"Get in the car and I will explain everything."

I don't budge. "Why should I trust you?"

"Please, Raven. This is important. I'm not going to hurt you."

"You already have."

"I know. I couldn't help it, but you have to hear me out."

I watch him for a few seconds, my eyes moving over his face, the intense expression and the desire for me that still emanates from his eyes.

I point an index finger at him. "If this turns out to just be about sex, I'm never speaking to you again. Got it?"

He nods once, his body rigid, as if he's holding his real thoughts in check. I'm used to the electricity between us, but this is more than that. This is serious. Me thinking it is about sex is wishful thinking.

Silently we walk to the car. He opens the front passenger door and I climb in. When he gets in, he does not look at me, but pulls away from the casino.

"Tell me what this is all about," I ask.

He shakes his head. "Not yet. I need to look into your eyes

when I tell you this. I need you to understand exactly what you need to do."

That chills me. I sit back, wringing my hands in my lap until they hurt. Not another word is spoken, and the atmosphere is so heavy it feels like the air before a tropical thunderstorm. It is obvious he's going to tell me something I'm not going to like. There's no other explanation for his silence or his sudden appearance outside of the casino. I will finally know exactly what he wants from me.

We pull into the apartment building's parking garage and walk together to the lift. I watch his reflection in the lift doors. He looks so distant. So unapproachable I cannot imagine this is the same man who has been inside my body. Once inside his apartment, he directs me to the leather couch and sits next to me. No drinks tonight. No sexually charged glances. I sit up a little straighter and prepare myself to hear the bad news. For bad news it definitely is.

He doesn't waste time trying to assure or soothe me, just jumps right into it. "The night when I found you in the alley, you wanted to know why I was at the party, right?"

I nod.

"I followed you there."

I scoot back on the couch further away from him. This isn't a huge surprise, of course, but it still hurts to know he lied. I swallow hard and pretend I'm not hurt, because clearly we haven't come to the worst part.

"Why?" I ask.

His jaw tightens. "I was hired to."

My jaw drops. "What? By who?"

He looks away from me and I mentally prepare myself for it to get even worse than I imagined.

"It doesn't matter by who. The less you know the safer you will be. Suffice to say he is a very powerful and brutal man. I have worked for him on a couple of occasions in the past. He hires me because he knows I always get the job done. I'm the best in the business, and I work for him because he pays my price."

My head is so blank the words almost don't make sense. What is he talking about?

His eyes burn into mine for a few seconds before he continues. "My assignment was to make contact with you and find out what you knew."

I frown, my eyebrows scrunching together. "What I knew? I don't understand. You must have me mixed up with someone else. I'm just a lowly croupier in a casino. I don't know *anything* that could help a man who is as powerful and brutal as you say he is."

"The man who hired me is the Don of one of the most powerful Russian mafia families in England."

I inhale sharply.

"The killer you saw outside of the casino six months ago is his son."

I recoil from Konstantin in horror, and stare at him in shock. He grasps my hands and I try to tug them free, but he only strengthens his grip, pinning me in place.

"Let go of me," I whisper. "I want to leave. I'll … I'll take the bus home."

"It's not so simple. You are no longer safe, Raven. There is a price on your head now."

Fear courses through my veins and I start struggling with all my might.

"Will you just stay still, Raven?"

His voice. This is my lover. The fight goes out of me. "Who are you?" I gasp.

"I'm a professional assassin, Raven. I was hired to find and eliminate you."

CHAPTER THIRTY

KONSTANTIN

27 years ago

https://www.youtube.com/watch?v=6TpyRE_juyA
(I blinked and you were not the same anymore)

The first I know that something is wrong is when my mother freezes. Her eyes find mine and in that moment the world stops spinning. There is nothing but me and her. Then the air is shattered by the sound of guns firing, and I watch the terror fly into her eyes. Suddenly she moves, so fast my jaw drops.

Outside, I hear men shouting. They are speaking in Serbian.

My mother lifts me from my chair, tucks me under her arm. Covering my mouth with her other hand she stuffs me into the cupboard where we keep our winter things. It smells of wool and mothballs. She puts her finger to her lips and says in the fiercest voice I ever heard her use, "Don't make a sound. Not one sound. No matter what happens you don't come out, do you hear me?"

I stare at her.

She shakes my shoulders so hard my teeth chatter. "Do you understand?"

I nod blankly.

"Promise?" she whispers.

"Promise," I whisper back.

"Not one small sound," she reminds again.

I nod.

Then she smiles, even though her mouth is trembling. "I love you so much," she says.

"I love you too, Mama."

"Hurry. They are almost here," my grandmother, who had been sitting half-asleep in her chair, cries.

"Now close your eyes and do not open them until the men are gone," my mother orders.

I nod and close my eyes. With my eyes closed I hear the door shut. As soon as I hear her footsteps move away I open my eyes. The door didn't close all the way. The wood is old and warped. There is a narrow crack. I lean forward and put one eye to the crack.

I see my grandmother stand from her chair. Her face is pale and frightened. "Quickly, cover your hair," she barks at my mother.

My mother grabs a scarf and ties it around her head. Then she runs her hands down her hips. I don't know why she's doing that. She only makes that action when her hands are wet. Straightening her back she starts walking to the table in the middle of the room where she was peeling potatoes and putting them into a bowl. The potatoes are for our dinner tonight.

Just as my mother reaches the table a soldier bursts into our home. My mother carries on walking until she is standing in front of grandma. "Take what you want. We are just two women here. Leave us be. Please," she says in Serbian.

The man stares at my mother, then he begins to laugh slowly. My mother never learnt to speak Serbian properly and her pronunciation is quite funny. Papa always laughs at her. The man must be laughing at her too.

"Please. There is money in that tin," my mother pleads. This time she even makes a mistake, but now her voice is shaking. Mama is scared of the man.

I want to open the cupboard and tell him to go away, but I am frozen. It is too late to close my eyes. I promised I would not make a sound. I wonder where Papa is. Or my brothers. Or even my grandfather. He is going deaf so maybe he didn't hear the gunshots.

Another soldier comes into the house. He does not speak. He walks up to my mother and grins.

"There is food and money. Take it all," my mother says.

He doesn't speak. He punches my mother so hard in the stomach she falls to the ground. I open my mouth to scream but no sound comes out. My mouth is wide open but no sound comes out.

"Keep your eyes closed, little bear. Keep them closed and don't make a sound,' my mother says in Bosnian.

But I can't. I can't close my eyes. I can't make a sound. I can't move. I am frozen.

"Don't look," she adds. "Don't look."

The soldier turns towards my grandmother. He lifts his gun and shoots her in the head. She falls. My mother screams and my whole world breaks apart.

Who are these men? Why did they kill my grandmother?

I don't understand what is going on. The man who shot Grandma grabs my mother by the hair and pulls her up. She cries out in pain. I feel my face grow warm and my hand clench. He is hurting Mama. I have to protect her.

"Don't come out. Don't come. And keep your eyes closed," my mother says again in Bosnian.

Roughly, he throws her on the table. The bowl of potatoes overturn. Potatoes go flying. One rolls all the way to the cupboard door. If I put my hand through the crack I can pick it up and throw it really hard at the man. As I stare at the potato I hear a tearing sound. My head jerks up.

I cannot see him. Only my mother. The man has torn her skirt. I can see her pale waist and some of her white underwear. I have never seen her in her underwear. She doesn't even dry them outside because she is too ashamed to let people see them. I have to stop the man.

"Don't come out. Be a good boy," my mother warns.

"Shut the fuck up," the man swears in Serbian.

He tears her underclothes. She winces with pain. She closes her eyes. A second later they fly open. My mother turns her face and looks in my direction. Her eyes fall on the crack between the doors. Tears fill her eyes.

"Good boy. That's my good boy," she mouths.

Suddenly her eyes widen and her face contorts. She clenches her teeth. The man starts grunting, and her whole body starts to move up and down along the table. She cannot hold back her cries of pain. My hand twitches towards the door. I need to do something. I need to help my mother.

"A promise is a promise forever," she says, as if she can see me.

Something truly horrible is happening to my mother. I can tell by the way blood is streaming from her lip because she has bitten it.

There is the sound of more boots hitting the floor. Another soldier arrives in the room.

"Fuck, don't leave a bloody mess for the rest of us, you animal," he says. He has a commanding voice.

He comes to stand by my mother and I see his face. He unzips his trousers and takes out his cuckoo bird. His cuckoo bird is big and red. Other men come into the room. They too make my mother's body slide along the table.

The only sounds she makes are to tell me how proud she is of me. To stay quiet. To not come out. To remind me of my promise. It seems to be hours that I am in that cupboard with the smell of mothballs and the men torturing my mother while I remain frozen with my eye to the crack.

"We'll kill all of you. We'll fucking kill all of you," a man says as he punches my mother and she falls to the floor. My mother doesn't move. A man kicks her in the stomach and she does not flinch.

Then they leave the house.

I hear them go out to the front, then the sound of their trucks rolling away, but I can't move. I wonder why Papa has not come in. Or my brothers. Or Grandad. Then I hear Mama gasping.

In the dead silence, I think I hear her call my name, but I can't be sure. I open the cupboard and try to take a step and fall. My legs won't work. I look at Mama. How strange. She is naked waist down and covered in blood, but she is blowing a spit bubble.

My head feels strange.

I hear it then. A gasping, choking sound. My mother is calling me. I sit up slowly. I feel as if I am floating above my body. I crawl to my mother. Something is wrong with her. Her body is contorted in the way that Wanda, our goat's was when she broke her hip bone. I crouch next to Mama. Her face and mouth is so swollen her eyes are slits.

Her lips move and she blows another bubble. It is tinged with red. She is saying something. I crouch over her and hold my ear over her mouth.

"Did you see the men?" she whispers.

"Only one," I whisper back.

"Avenge me."

I turn my head and stare at her. I don't know what she means. I haven't learnt the meaning of this word yet.

"Avenge me," she repeats, and tears flow out of her eyes.

I don't know what she is asking, but I know it is very important. I nod. "I will."

"Now. Do to me what you did to Mishka," she croaks, and blood pours out of her mouth.

I stare at her, horrified.

"Hurry. I cannot bear the pain any longer."

"I can't, Mama. Don't leave me, please," I cry.

"The angels are waiting for me, Konstantin,' she begs, and looks at me with eyes so pitiful something inside me tears open.

"You must do it now," she urges.

I lean forward, my hands trembling, and smother her face with my hands. I pinch her nose and lay my hand over her mouth, but I can see her eyes. They look at me until the light goes out of them.

There are no tears in my eyes. No pain in my heart. I stand slowly. I'm six years old, but my mother's soul has passed out through my hands and I feel as if I am ten feet tall and giddy, giddy with a strange emotion. I took my own mother's life. The life of the person I loved most in this world.

I pass my grandmother without looking at her and walk out of the front door.

Outside, I see my father lying on the ground in a pool of red. Dead. And a few feet away, my brothers. Also dead. I loved them all dearly. But I feel nothing. No pain. No horror.

I just walk. And walk. And walk. And walk.

My hands are covered in blood. My clothes are covered in blood. I walk down the stony path. The two goats are lying on the ground. Their bodies are still.

I know only one thing. It burns my brain. Obliterates everything else. There is nothing else. But the need to hurt my mother's attackers.

I must find those men.

They have killed my family.

Now I must kill them all.

CHAPTER THIRTY-ONE

RAVEN

https://www.youtube.com/watch?v=-rC8RRXcfeo
(Stay With Me)

*T*he strength goes out of me. He lets go of my hands and I collapse against the back of the couch, gulping air that won't come fast enough. My mind refuses to believe what I have just heard. Things like this don't happen to ordinary people. I am an ordinary person. The only thing a bit unusual about me is my name. Other than that I have to be the most ordinary person in the world.

"No," I gasp in disbelief. My head is shaking. "No, no, no. I don't believe it. You're Serbian. I've read about the Russian mafia. You can't just enter it. How could you be in the Russian mafia?"

"I didn't say I was in the Russian mafia. I have nothing to do with them. I am a professional assassin. I work for anyone who is willing to pay my price."

I stare at him in completely shock "That's your job? You actually kill people for money?"

His eyes are expressionless. "Yes."

"And your assignment was me?"

"Yes."

"I don't understand. Why hire you? Why not just ask one of the goons I saw that night or even his son? It looked to me like he actually enjoyed killing that man."

"His son is a hot-headed fool. He shouldn't even have been in that alley. A decade ago both you and Cindy would already be dead, but the Don has been under increased police surveillance for some time now so he cannot afford to order a hit unless absolutely necessary, and if he does he has to be extremely careful there is no blow back. Using a hitman with no links to their organization is a practical solution. My assignment was to find out which one of you was in the alley that night and take her out, but if you had not seen his son's face he would have been willing to allow you to live."

I look at him in confusion. "But how did they even know anyone was there? They didn't see me and I made no sound at all." My voice is suddenly small and shaky. I never saw this coming. Not in a million years could I have imagined that Konstantin was a hired gun sent to kill me.

"You made two mistakes. You didn't leave enough time before you went back to the casino. They heard the sound of the door and returned, and when they did they found the electricity bill you dropped."

"Our electricity bill?" My mind whirls. I can barely scrape my thoughts together so they'll make sense. The stupid electricity bill! That's how they found me. That's why I couldn't find it. I tucked it into the sleeve of my purse to remind me to pay it in the morning, and it fell out while I was trying to get back into the casino. "But all this happened six months ago. Why now?"

"In less than a month the Don's son goes on trial for a minor financial irregularity. Everything has been arranged so he will get off with only a caution, but there could be some media coverage. Maybe a photo and a few inches of ink buried in the middle of a couple of broadsheets. Unfortunately, that opens up the possibility that you could see the article and recognize him. They can't take that chance."

"I don't even read the papers," I wail.

He shrugs. "You could see it in the paper used to wrap the fish and chips you buy on a Friday night."

"They don't use newspapers to wrap fish and chips anymore," I say automatically.

"You know what I mean. Someone could be reading a paper in the casino. Your father could leave his papers open. Someone could tell you about it."

I lift my hand up. "I get it. He wants to take care of the billion in one chance that I see the photograph of his precious son that might not even be printed."

"Exactly."

"How much money are you getting for … eliminating me?"

He doesn't flinch. "I don't work for less than $250,000.00"

My eyes widen and I start to babble, words streaming out of my mouth. "250,000 dollars? Come on! For a big Don he sure didn't get his money's worth. He could have had me killed for a lot less money. I watched a documentary the other day where a man killed a woman for £5000. Cash. He should have gone to him. Much cheaper."

"There is a lot of planning that goes into these kinds of jobs. I had to arrange surveillance, rent this place, cars. You watched that documentary because the man was caught. I will never get caught and the hit will never be linked to the Don."

I take a deep breath. "You're the Rolls Royce of the elimination game, huh?"

"Yes."

"Is that where you were these last few days? Reporting back to headquarters? Deciding how to murder me. Telling this … this criminal all about the stupid girl you took to the castle and fucked … because hey, might as well have some fun before you ice her, right?"

"No," he roars.

"So all this was just some job to you?" I ask, my voice dead and defeated.

"No," he says immediately, but doesn't elaborate, which infuriates me even more.

"Why should I believe you? Everything between us has been a lie. You used me," I accuse bitterly.

He shakes his blond head once, his lips pressing into an unhappy line. "I didn't use you, Raven. Never."

"That's funny, because from where I'm sitting it sure feels that way. What was the plan?"

He pales and looks away. "It was supposed to look like an accident."

"What kind of accident?"

He turns toward me. "Does it matter?"

"Yes, damnit it does. I'd like to know how you plan to kill me."

"Don't be a fool. If I wanted to kill you, you'd already be dead. You are not simply a job." He stops and swallows. "You never were. I ... uh ... care for you."

"Wow. Lucky me," I say sarcastically, because I'm so hurt. I ... uh ... care for you? That's what he feels for me? I glare at him.

He looks down at his hands.

"So what happens now?"

"He knows my methods. I told him I'd coaxed the information out of you, and I assured him that you did not see his son's face."

It takes a moment to get words out of my stunned mind. My voice is barely a whisper. "You lied to the Don?"

"Yes."

"Why did you do that? I'm just an assignment. Another quarter of a million into what sounds like a numbered Swiss bank account."

He caresses my face, his long fingers gentle on my cheek, and I don't pull away. I can't. In fact, it takes all I have not to melt at that moment.

"You know why."

"Tell me."

"I, because I ... I ... care ... for you."

I close my eyes. He feels it. I know he feels it. He just can't say it. "So why did you say I was still in danger?"

He drops his hand from my cheek, the look on his face the same forlorn one I saw that night in the castle when he thought he was alone. I want to comfort him, this cold-hearted contract killer who was supposed to end my life, but somehow, cares about me too much to do it. I might have been wrong about everything else, but I wasn't wrong about our connection.

"When I told him there was no reason to kill you, since you didn't know anything, he laughed at me and suggested that my technique might be slipping. He thought you had lied to me, because his moles in the police department told him otherwise. One of them recently gained access to the original casefile. He saw that not only had you admitted seeing the face of the man with the gun, but you were so sure you could recognize him again you looked through the department's mugshots. Basically, he wanted me to finish the job as per our contract. Without you there can be no case against his son."

The rug gets pulled from under me again. "Does this mean you still have to kill me?"

A look of such sadness crosses his face that I want to hold him close to my heart. "I would never hurt you, Raven. Or take you away from Janna. I know what it is to be alone in the world."

"So what do we do? Run?" Thoughts whizz at the speed of light through my mind. Janna. Cindy. Mum. Dad. My job at the casino. The Russian mafia boss who wants me dead.

He shakes his head slowly. "Not we, Raven. You. You need to leave the country. If you do not disappear completely, he will send someone else to kill you. The nature of their business makes these kinds of men suffer huge paranoia, Raven. He will never stop until you are dead, and once he knows I took his money and crossed him I will also become a target."

I shiver suddenly. It feels like an icy block just settled in the pit of my stomach.

"Are you cold?" he asks, reaching for me.

I sink into his arms, craving that closeness, that familiar heat. My head is spinning too quickly to form coherent thoughts. I can't think of the first thing to do. Go to the police? No, they can't be trusted. Run? Sure, but where? And with what money? I just want to forget. Just for a minute. I want to lose myself in him. To pretend for a while we are still at the castle and we are just a man and a woman who cannot bear for our skins to be parted even for a minute. The truth is, despite all the lies, secrets and deceit, I still desperately want to kiss him, and climb into his lap.

I tip my head up and fuse my lips with his.

His mouth opens. My tongue pushes in and I scoot closer as my hands claw and rip his shirt open roughly. Buttons fly. This is the only thing I can trust. Our coupling. The rest of the world will wait. I push his shirt away and let my hands loose on that warm, smooth skin. Without breaking the kiss my hands reach for his belt. I undo it and pull the elastic of his underpants. His cock springs out, hard as rock.

His big strong hands lift me up bodily as he pulls at my panties. He drags them down my legs. Pulling his mouth away from mine, he lifts me up over his lap, and impales me on his cock.

"Yes," I gasp.

"God, I've missed you so much," he whispers in my hair.

"Me too."

"My name is not Konstantin. It's Dragan. Say my name."

"Dragan," I whisper.

"Say it again," he whispers urgently.

I repeat his name.

With a groan, he rolls me onto the couch, and thrusts hard into me. Our coming together is frantic and urgent as if we are in a race against the blackness that is about to overcome us. Neither of us lasts. The second I go over, he lets himself explode too. Hard. Calling my name. Our breaths mingle. I want to find a way to stay in this moment—the two of us joined together. Here I am safely protected from the rest of the world, and the threat of the contract out on my head seems a long way away.

"I love you, Dragan," I sob.

He doesn't say it back. "I'm sorry, Raven. I'm so sorry."

I close my eyes for a second and feel him pull out of me, and move away. I open my eyes and watch him as he zips up his trousers.

"Let me clean you up," he says softly, and walks away.

I lie there in a daze. He comes back with a wet towel. Gently, the way I used to clean Janna when she was a baby, he wipes me and closes my legs.

"You must leave in the morning," he says. "Begin a new life in another country."

Tears fill my eyes. "Why can't we go with you?"

He shakes. "No. Not with me. The way I live." He shakes his head. "It's not for you and Janna."

I throw myself at his chest. "How do you know?"

"I am a man with no fixed address, no nationality, no family, no friends. I'm like the wind. You see me here today, and I look solid and real to you, but if you try to look for me tomorrow, it will be like looking for something that doesn't exist. Everything I have is fake, rented, or temporary."

"I don't care about that. You are real."

He shakes his head sadly. "You didn't even know my name until a few minutes ago."

"What are you saying? This is it? I never see you again?"

"It is better that way. Safer. For both you and Janna. You have to listen to me. These men are ruthless. They will not hesitate to silence you and the child."

"Where will I go? I have no money and nowhere to go? I know no one who can help."

He puts his large hands on my shoulders and pulls me close to his face. "I have prepared everything for you and Janna. Money, papers with new names, tickets, cover story. Your first destination will be Paris. After that you can decide for yourself if you want to stay, or leave for somewhere else, but what is important is that you will leave this country and never look back."

"This is why you went away. To prepare all this for me?"

He nods.

"What about my life here?" I whisper. I'm too stunned to cry. Too shocked to do anything but hang on to his thighs, blinking and struggling to control the sick roiling in my stomach.

"Raven. Everyone knows who you are. Where you work. Where you live." He pauses to let this sink in, his beautiful eyes steady. "You cannot remain here and be safe. Staying in this country is not an option. You have to follow the plan I provide to the letter or everything will unravel."

"Okay," I whisper.

"Listen carefully."

I nod and he begins outlining the plan that will take me away from everything I've ever known.

CHAPTER THIRTY-TWO

DRAGAN

https://www.youtube.com/watch?v=MBNebfsKlR0
(My Oh My)

I drop her at home and drive away without looking
in the rearview mirror. I don't want to look. My
hands clench the steering wheel hard, but against my will my
eyes flick upwards. She is standing at the side of the road,
clutching the thick envelope I gave her, and watching my car
speed away. She looks so small and vulnerable.

God, her face is so white.

I tell myself that it is better this way, but terrible pain radiates out of my chest. I haven't felt any emotions since that
day I suffocated my own mother. The pain throbs and burns.
She is mine and I've just let her go. I can't have her. What
kind of life would it be for her and the child? My fist slams
on the steering wheel in frustration.

I press the pedal to the floor and the car screeches forward. I go through one set of red lights, but the streets of London are not meant for speeding. There are too many cars and people about. I slow down and take deep breaths to try and calm my racing heart.

A man with a dog crosses the street in front of me. I watch him and his body language. He loves his pet. I never understood love before.

I did the right thing. I wanted to keep her so badly, it hurt like nothing before had, but I can't be selfish and ruin her life. She will be safer the further away she is from me. I am used to being alone. I'm better alone. I was fine before her and I will be fine again. I will have nothing in my life but my work. I will do my job with great efficiency and I will get paid for it. There is simplicity in that. No one can kill better than me. It is a special skill to see someone in your telescopic sight, aim, fire, watch the target go down and feel nothing. I will go back to being the most efficient killing machine on earth.

The pain remains lodged in my chest.

I don't know what the future holds. It depends on her. If she can stay hidden. If she thinks there are no more dangers, and reaches out to one of her friends, or goes to see her parents. If she forgets or gets careless, and calls them on their birthdays.

I know going against Sergei is pure madness, only a suicidal fool would attempt it, but I'd rather look behind my shoulder for the rest of my life or die like a dog in some alleyway, a bullet to my head, than harm one hair on that woman's head. She is a pure and innocent soul, and saving her is the best thing I've done in my life. She is the woman I would have chosen if I was a different man, in a different life.

I return to my apartment.

For the first time since I moved in, I notice that my apartment looks cold and soulless. My hands are twitching and my whole body feels restless. I go into my training room, strip down, and start to work out. As I am punching the heavy bag I force my mind to remain blank. There is nothing but that black bag swinging from the ceiling and my fists connecting hard with it. I stop when my chest is heaving and my muscles are screaming and the floor underneath me is so wet my feet are slipping. I look up to the mirror. My face is red and sweat is running down my body in rivulets.

I can do this without her.

I can start again.

Raven? She was just a mistake. I shouldn't even have taken the assignment. It was a favor to a friend and it has cost me dearly. I am not the man I was.

Raven has all the paperwork necessary to get out of the country, the train tickets, the envelope of unmarked bills, and the bankcard for an account I set up in her new name. Money will never be an issue for her again. She and Janna will have all they need. They will be happy.

I must find solace in that.

As soon as I confirm the train has carried Raven and Janna safely out of the city, I will go to Sergei, show him the photo of Raven with her chest covered in pig's blood, and tell him the job is done. Then, I will carry on with my old life. I will forget Raven and Janna ever existed. That way, I will keep them safe. In time she will move on. She will forget me.

My absence is their only chance at survival.

CHAPTER THIRTY-THREE

RAVEN

*I*t is Cindy's night off and she is asleep on the couch with Janna. I watch them for a long time, feeling numb with shock. When I feel a sob rise up my throat, I hold my hand over my mouth to keep from waking them. I love them both so much.

Leaving everything behind means leaving her too.

How can I leave Cindy behind?

She's more than a friend and roommate. She's a sister to me. I don't know what I would have done without her after Octavia passed away. She kept me sane and focused. She gave me a break, watching Janna when I needed a few minutes to fall apart. I love her. The way Konstantin, no, Dragan, drummed it into my head. I have to walk away forever. That means the only time we can meet is in secret in another country, after we have agreed to the meeting using encrypted messages in Internet shops.

I gently shake her shoulder. Her eyes open slowly and she

blinks up at me. It takes a few seconds for her to fully step out of her dreams.

"Raven?" She sits up a little, rubbing her eyes as she carefully extricates herself from Janna's little arms. "What's wrong?"

I sink to the floor, just drop to my butt where I stand. First she frowns, then she joins me on the floor. I tell her everything in a blur of tears and whispers. Konstantin's real identity. The mob boss who wants me dead. The plan to keep Janna and me safe. Cindy stares at me, her eyes round with horror and astonishment. I'm sure it must seem to her that she is still dreaming. Finally, her arms go around me and she leans her head against mine.

"We have to leave tomorrow," I tell her. "Our train is scheduled to pull out of the station at ten-thirty."

She lifts her head, startled. "Tomorrow?"

I nod. "He gave me everything. Passports with fake names, money, train tickets, a believable cover story."

"So you're leaving tomorrow?" she repeats in wonder.

"I don't want to leave, Cin."

She frowns. "All of this is so incredible it sounds like something from a movie."

"I can't believe it myself," I admit.

"There must be some other way."

I shake my head. "He says if the Don even suspects that he has been double-crossed he will hunt me and Dragan down."

"God. What a mess!"

"The worst part is I'm not even supposed to tell Mum and

Dad because these people might go around to them. The only way they will be safe is if they think we've both just disappeared, but I can't devastate Mum like that. I couldn't live with myself if I did that to her. She'll go mad with worry. After we've gone I want you to tell Mum everything. She can make something up for Dad. With his dementia, he can barely remember what he ate yesterday so it won't really matter. Mum's good at keeping secrets so I'm not worried that she'll blab to the neighbors or something."

Without warning Cindy starts crying, her tears making me feel even worse. Tough Cindy. The last time I saw her cry was when her dog died and that was fifteen years ago.

"How could this happen to you?" she whispers, clinging to me as I cling to her.

We both turn to look at sweet Janna asleep on the couch at the same time. She is completely oblivious to the total meltdown happening in front of her. If I do this, that will leave us alone, just the two of us against the world. But if I stay and something happens to me, she'll be by herself. I can't let her lose me. I promised Octavia I'd take care of her until she was grown up.

"He told me to pack what I need for one night," I say in an almost calm voice. Now that I've cried my eyes out, that stunned feeling is back. "A single small bag for each of us. Nothing that would draw the attention of our neighbors, or make it seem like we are going away. We have to leave before the sun rises and stay hidden until it's time for us to board." I glance at my watch. I have to keep to the plan.

Cindy hugs me harder, her breath hitching. "My aunt is out of town for another week. You can stay at her place until your train leaves. You've never been to her new apartment so no one will recognize you there. She's letting me use her car too. It's downstairs, so we won't have to risk taking a taxi." Now that she's let out her tears, she's all business.

"No, that is not the plan. Any change in the plan will make it unravel."

She stands and drags me to my feet. "Fine. I get it. Come on. Let's get a couple of bags packed for you and Janna."

I follow her, doing what she tells me to do, my insides numb, my head cluttered with unfinished thoughts that don't make any sense. I ache to see Dragan. All I want to do is go back to his cold flat and ask him to hold me. I wish there was some way out of this situation, but I know in my heart that if there was, he would have thought of it. He knows this Don. If he says he's a danger to Janna and me, then I believe him.

We fill a backpack for Janna and a duffel bag for me with a few clothes and some personal items—a family photo album, Janna's well-worn, favorite teddy bear. Dragon emphasized the importance of leaving things like toiletries, my purse with money and credit cards, and my passport and driving license behind. Taking them would make the police think we hadn't simply disappeared in the night, but had left of our own accord. What the police knew the Don's moles would report back.

"Okay, let's go through the story you tell everyone, including the police," I tell Cindy.

She quickly runs through the story Dragan concocted for us. She was asleep in her room. When she woke up we had gone. Unfortunately, she didn't hear anything, because she is a very heavy sleeper. I had not mentioned wanting to go away again. Yes, I went on the weekend with a man, but she has no idea who he is or where he lives.

Then, I take one final tour of the apartment where the three of us have lived for the last few years, our personalities on every wall, our memories echoing in every item. We'll make new memories, the two of us. We'll have to.

I go back to the living room where we have not switched on the light. "Okay, I'm ready."

We reach for each other at the same time and hug so hard it hurts. Both of us sniffling into each other's ears to keep the tears back. I don't know what to say to her. I can't remember a time in my life when I didn't know this woman. She's walked with me through everything. After tonight I don't know when I'll see her again, or even if I will.

"Be safe, Raven, and take care of our little girl."

I nod instead of answering, not trusting myself to hold it together.

"I'll go to the internet café and set up that email address first thing in the morning so you'd better find a moment to tell me you're okay, real quick."

"I will," I promise, holding on tight.

We rock each other back and forth the way we have done for years.

"I wish you were coming with us," I say, only half joking.

Cindy pulls away from me. "I'll find you again," she promises, pressing her forehead against mine. "This isn't goodbye. It's see you soon."

I nod. "Okay. See you soon. I love you."

"Love you too." I let her go, but I don't budge. Neither does she.

"What if I can't do this?"

She presses her palms on either side of my cheeks and looks deep into my eyes. "You can do this. Rosa always said you don't look it, but of all of us, you are the strongest."

We watch each other for a long, drawn out moment, our eyes taking in the other's face, committing it to memory for later.

I pick Janna up from the couch. She is so deeply asleep, she doesn't do much more than whimper and burrow into my shoulder. I walk to the front door with Cindy following behind. I stop to turn around. "I love you, Cin. Always remember that."

She can't say the words. She just nods, her chin trembling. Then she leans forward and kisses Janna's cheek.

"Bye," I whisper.

She nods again and opens the door and stands behind it just in case someone passes by and sees her. No one must know that she was awake during the night. I step out of our home, and she closes the door behind us. I walk quickly and quietly. It's past three in the morning so the corridors are empty.

We make it out of the building without incident or meeting anyone. I walk around the block and see the white Honda with the number plates Dragan made me memorize waiting for me. I bundle Janna into the car and the driver immediately pulls away from the kerb. I turn around and look back.

The street is empty.

It seems incredible to think that I will never be coming back here.

CHAPTER THIRTY-FOUR

RAVEN

*M*orning takes a long time to come, but finally, sunlight shines into the windows of the bare room where Janna and I are curled up on a bed. She slept through the night, unaware of the complete upheaval our lives have been through. I couldn't sleep at all. I just kept going over the plan, trying to count the contingencies like sheep until sleep overcame me, but I was too wired up to fall asleep.

Janna's eyelids flutter open, as if on cue. She rubs her eyes and looks around her. "Where's my room, Mummy?"

"We had a sleepover at a friend's house, darling."

She frowns. "Whose house is this?"

I touch her button nose. "Just a friend."

She yawns and stretches, unconcerned to be waking up in a completely strange environment.

"We have to get dressed and have breakfast, okay, munchkin?"

"Are we having pancakes?"

"Again? You can't have pancakes every day. Choose between scrambled or boiled eggs."

She leans her face on the palm of her hand. "Scrambled," she decides.

"Cool. And guess what we're doing after breakfast?"

"Are we going to the park?"

I pretend to grin. I don't want to alarm Janna in the slightest. She needs to think we are on a great adventure. "Nope. Even better than that. We're going on a special trip today."

"Where to?" she asks, her face animated.

"Guess?"

"To Konstantin's castle," she shouts.

"That was not Konstantin's castle I went to. I told you he rented it for the weekend."

"But a Prince has to live in a castle."

"Konstantin is not a Prince."

She giggles. "He is, silly. He's a secret prince, and you're going to be a secret Princess,"

My heart feels as if it is breaking. "You're the silly one, kiddo."

"You are," she counters immediately.

"Anyway, we're not going to a castle." I widen my eyes as if I'm telling her the most exciting thing in the world. "We're going to Paris!"

Her eyes become round and her mouth opens in wonder. "Paris!"

I nod. "We have to get on a high-speed train to get there."

"Weeeee," she squeals excitedly. "What will we do in Paris, Mummy?"

"We can do whatever we like."

A huge smile blooms on her face. "Is Aunty Cindy coming?" she asks.

What will she do without her Auntie Cindy? I keep my expression bright. "Not this time, kiddo," I say softly. "Now, let's go get some breakfast. I can hear your stomach growling like a beast in the night."

*T*he same man who picked us up in the early hours of the morning drives us to the train station. He has his radio on and none of us talk. Even Janna, which is unlike her. She seems content to look out the window, completely unaware of how terrified I am. The car comes to a stop outside St Pancras station.

"If you want I can park the car and go in with you?"

Hearing him speak startles me. I whirl my head around to face him. His dark eyes are shiny and calm. It occurs to me to ask him for his contact number. He must know how to contact Dragan. Then I hear Dragan's urgent voice. *Any attempt to contact me will only endanger you and Janna.*

I shake my head. "No, I don't think so. Thank you for your offer."

He nods solemnly.

I grab my duffel bag and we get out of the car and he drives off. Standing at the entrance I fit Janna's green and blue backpack on her shoulders.

"Ready?" I ask.

She nods vigorously and we walk into the station.

"Look at this place, munchkin," I exclaim, looking up at the lofty, curving glass roof.

She gives a little skip of excitement. How lovely to be so innocent, so unaware of hurt, pain, betrayal or fear of the unknown.

I clutch my bag tightly. Everything I own in the world is in it. A fat envelope with the tickets, our new passports, cash, and bankcards with my new name on it. Kelly Moore. He didn't tell me how much was in the account he set up, just that we'd never have to worry about money again. The thought is dizzying.

I glance down at her as we move through the crowd. She is looking ahead of her, mesmerized by so much frantic activity. I check the board of arrivals and departures to find our platform.

We walk towards the platform; Janna is quiet as she drinks in the sight of the high-speed train. She hasn't ridden one before. We've never had the money for holidays, even small ones. Once we get on it and the train leaves the station, our new lives begin. We just have to pass the barrier, walk along the platform and climb up the steps into the train.

"Why are we waiting here?" Janna asks.

I stare at the shiny new train.

Janna tugs on my arm when I don't answer right away.

"Mummy?"

I look down at her. She is staring up at me with a questioning look. "Aren't we going into the train?"

"Yes, honey, of course we are."

"Then why are we waiting here?"

I stare down at her. I'm all she's got. I've to put her first. I can't be selfish. I prepare to take the first step, but my foot won't move. I look down at Janna and smile a we're-going-on-a-great-adventure smile. Then I straighten my spine and look up. I can do this. I have to do this. I take a deep breath. At that instant two women on the other side of the platform walk into my vision. Their entire bodies are concealed under black niqabs, nothing is visible but their eyes.

The sight is like a bolt of lightning. It is as if I have been in a daze all this while and have just woken up.

I look down at Janna. "This is not our train, darling. I made a mistake. Our train is later. It might even be tomorrow."

Janna makes a disappointed noise, her little face scrunching into a frown. "Awwww."

"Don't worry though you're going to do something even more fun today." Turning away from the train, and bringing her around with me, I walk briskly towards the mouth of the other platform. I slow my steps as I approach the women and smile to appear less crazy than I'm sure I'm about to sound.

"Hello," I greet.

Both women look at each other then the younger one returns the greeting. "Good morning." Her voice is polite, but her kohl-rimmed, dark eyes are suspicious. I guess not many strangers talk to women like her.

I take a deep breath. "This is going to sound really insane, but you wouldn't happen to have another headscarf you'd be willing to sell to me, would you?"

She stares at me without answering. I can't see her face to gauge her reaction to what I've just said, but her eyes suddenly dart to the left of me. I'm sure she's thinking about walking away and escaping from me.

"Please. I'm in trouble," I plead, lowering my voice to keep from drawing Janna's attention. "I need to cover my face. I can't say much more than that. I'm willing to pay cash. Just name your price."

The woman blinks her large eyes, then glances down at Janna before looking up at me again. "You ... and the baby are in danger?"

I nod. "Yes. I need a way to cover my face."

The other woman says something in Arabic. I recognize it instantly from working at the casino. The younger woman explains and the older woman stares at me.

"Why are they dressed like that, Mummy?" Janna asks.

"It's their religion, darling," I say, smiling awkwardly at the older woman.

She considers me for a moment longer before nodding and pointing to the bag she is carrying and saying something else in Arabic.

"We can give you one of our spare ones," the younger woman says.

"That's wonderful," I gush, reaching eagerly for my purse. "How much?"

She shakes her head, her striking eyes soft with kindness. "I won't take your money."

Unexpectedly, my eyes fill with tears. All my life I have looked at these women in their black robes and felt they must be a species altogether different from me. I even secretly looked down on them. They had given away their rights. And now in my hour of greatest need it is one of them who has stepped up to help me.

"Come, I will help you put it on in the bathroom."

She picks up her bag and we follow the two women to the restroom. While Janna watches, entranced by the two women, the younger woman opens one of their small suitcase and removes a long black robe and veil from it. She holds them out to me and I take the niqab. They smell strongly of perfume. I smile at her and she smiles back. I can tell she is by the crinkles around her eyes.

I know the word for thank you in Arabic. "*Shukran*," I say.

She smiles at me warmly. "It is a pleasure."

"Are you sure I can't pay you for these scarves?"

She shakes her head. "Keep your little one safe. That's payment enough."

Before I can say another word, she picks up her bag and both women silently leave the bathroom.

It's only then that I realize I never asked her name.

CHAPTER THIRTY-FIVE

RAVEN

"**W**hy are you covering your face, Mummy?" Janna asks curiously.

"I'm just seeing what it would feel like. Sometimes it's good to walk in other people's shoes."

I take off the niqab and stuff it into my bag. Then I lift Janna from her perch on the countertop beside the sinks and put her on the ground. Holding her hand, I go out of the bathroom in search of a payphone. With Janna singing to herself, I dial the number that Star gave me. Five rings later and I start to pray. Please Star, pick up, pick up.

"Hello," a man answers.

For a second I think I have called the wrong number, but the man has a Russian accent, so I plough on. "Can I speak to Star, please?"

"Who is calling?"

"It's her old friend, Raven."

"Hold on one moment, please." I hear a couple of clicks then Star's voice comes on.

"Hi, Raven, how wonderful to hear from you." Her voice is surprised, but happy.

"Hey, Star. Remember you said if I ever needed help I should come to you."

"Yes."

"Do you still want to?"

"Absolutely. I'd love to help you in any way I can," she says immediately.

"Is this phone line secure?"

"Yes," she says, her tone serious.

"I need you to take care of Janna for a while, but the thing is you cannot let anyone know that she is with you. You cannot tell anyone that I have been in contact, or that you have seen me. And if you hear that I am missing you cannot offer any information, or tell anyone that you have seen or heard from me. This is extremely important. If you think you cannot do this then you cannot help me."

She inhales sharply. "What is going on, Raven?"

"I'll explain everything later, but first I need you to come get Janna now."

"Where are you?"

"At St Pancras station."

"I can get there in thirty minutes."

"Great." I look around me. "There's a little store selling Cornish pastries called McConnels. I'll be waiting there. I don't have my phone so don't try to call me. If you don't make it in half-an-hour I'll call you back."

"I'm leaving right now."

"Thanks, Star."

I hang up and take Janna to a little coffee shop. She's not hungry but I buy her a croissant and a hot chocolate. I watch her blow at her drink.

"So, darling," I say. "Do you remember Star? We met her for lunch at the Thai restaurant."

She nods. "Yeah. She has Princess hair."

I smile. "Yes, that's her. Well, you're going to be spending the day with her."

She stops chewing and looks a bit worried. "Just me?"

"Well, I'm going to be busy for a bit so she is going to take you to her house. She lives in a beautiful house. Actually, I think Aunty Cindy told me that she has horses too. Maybe she will let you see them, hmmm? What do you think?"

She thinks about it. "How long will you be?"

"A few hours at the most."

"Is that like two hours?"

"Something like that. Not long anyway."

"Okay."

How quickly she has forgotten our big adventure. I smile at her.

"Does Star have ponies?"

"I'm not sure, but you can ask her when she comes okay?"

"Okay." She pauses a moment, a considering expression on her face. "Can I have ice-cream now?"

"Sure," I agree.

"And chocolate too?" she asks eagerly.

"Janna, don't you think you're going a bit over the top now?"

She looks down at her croissant and tears off a bit, her face sad.

"All right. You can have the chocolate too, but that's all."

She looks up and beams at me.

I look at my watch. I have another twenty minutes to kill.

❄

I see Star hurrying towards us, the big guy in the suit following closely behind, and I start walking towards her.

"Are you all right?" she asks with a frown.

"Yeah, I'm fine."

"Does Cindy know you're here?"

"No."

She frowns. "What on earth is going on, Raven?"

I swivel my eyes towards Janna to indicate I don't want to discuss it in front of the child. "I just need you to keep Janna for a few hours."

"Yuri can take Janna to that shop and get her a little toy or a sweet?"

I nod.

She turns to the big guy who had stopped a few feet away from us. "Sure," he says walking towards us.

"Janna, this is Yuri. He's going to take you to buy a toy from that shop there. Would you like a toy?"

Janna nods then turns towards me. "Can I, Mummy?"

I smile. "Of course you can."

As soon as Yuri leads Janna away Star turns to me. "What the hell is going on?"

I tell her as briefly as I can and she shakes her head in astonishment. "Jesus, Raven, this is incredible. You must be so afraid. What are you going to do now?" she asks.

"I'm going to go and look for him."

"Is that really a good idea?"

"Look. I don't expect you to understand and at this moment it doesn't matter if you do or you don't. You said you'd help me and the only thing I need from you right now is for you to take care of Janna for me. Just for a few hours."

She sighs. "Okay. Got it, but remember that anytime at all you need help just call me immediately. Even if I can't help I'm pretty certain Nikolai will be able to. He's Russian and they all tend to know each other."

"Okay. I'll remember that."

From the corner of my eyes I can see Yuri and Janna coming back. She has a brown teddy bear tucked under her arm and she is happily munching on her second bar of chocolate today.

I kiss both Janna's rosy cheeks goodbye.

"Take care of her," I say to Star, feeling tearful to be leaving Janna.

"I will. Just take care of yourself."

When they have walked away I rush back to the bathroom, put on my heavily perfumed niqab, and make my way out of the station. I hop into one of the black taxis idling in front of the station.

I reach over, pull the door shut, and give the cabbie my address. To my surprise, he gives me a funny look, almost disgusted before he puts his eyes back on the road and pulls away. It takes me a full moment to realize it is the way I am dressed.

Fortunately, there is not much traffic on the road and the taxi pulls up across the street from the ground floor entrance of Dragan's apartment building. I hope and pray he is in. I don't know what I will do if he is not.

I pay my fare and climb out.

As I cross the street I have no idea how this is going to work out. How he will react to seeing me again. Nervously I approach the building, but as I get closer to the main entrance a woman opens the door from inside and comes out. I sprint for it and manage to catch it seconds before the catch closes. I view that as a good omen. Maybe the Gods are with me today.

The foyer is deserted. I cross it and take the elevator up to Dragan's floor. Again, there is no one around and I walk down the corridor to the closed door of his apartment. I take a deep breath and knock on his door. He's not going to be happy to see me, but his plan isn't going to work for me. I have the beginning of a new one that I'd like to run by him. It's one that gets us more of what we both want.

No one answers.

Out of mindless desperation and frustration I start banging on the door and calling out.

I know I shouldn't, but I pull my cellphone out of my purse and call him. A recording lets me know that the number has been disconnected. Feeling suddenly hot, sweaty and overwhelmed by the cloying perfume of the veil around my face and head I bang even harder on his door. Of course, I already know he is not in, but I'm just not ready to give in yet. I can't. This can't be the end.

"Why on earth are you making that bloody racket?" someone asks rudely.

I spin around to find a woman in her sixties or seventies poking her head out of an apartment several doors down. Her expression is hard and unfriendly.

"I'm looking for the man who lives here."

"What do you want with him?" she asks suspiciously as if I am a robber or a terrorist.

"He is my friend."

"If he is your friend then you should know he's gone," she says smugly.

"Gone?" I repeat in a daze.

"Yes, he moved out this morning. I saw the supervisor in there taking inventory," she replies, oblivious to the panic in my voice.

My head spins with shock. "Where can I find a forwarding address for him?"

"Try the supervisor," she suggests, and retreating back into her flat, quickly closes her door.

I collapse against the door to Dragan's old apartment and slide, defeated, to the floor. All the frenzied strength that carried me from the train station dissipates into nothing. I know there is no point asking the supervisor. Dragan warned me that looking for him would be the same as looking for the wind.

He has kept to the original plan, both of us disappearing from the city at the same time, going our separate ways, our paths never to cross again.

Oh God! No!

I'll never see him again.

CHAPTER THIRTY-SIX

RAVEN

https://www.youtube.com/watch?v=UJ8RBj_P0KQ
(Can't Help Falling In With You)

I don't know how long I remain slumped outside his door, lost and hopeless. I should have asked the driver this morning for his contact. Maybe I can find out from the people who rented out the castle. My hands clench. I've been so stupid. I don't even know how to get back to the moors. Then a weird thing happens. I don't believe in ghosts or aliens or anything supernatural, but I suddenly know where he is. It is not a guess. It is actually a knowing. As if my suffering soul whispered it to my heart.

Suddenly, re-energized, I jump to my feet and race down the corridor.

I hail a cab, get in and tell them the general direction. He had taken me at night, but it is as if I am guided by angels. We take a wrong turn once and I immediately 'feel' that we are on the wrong road and I tell the driver to go back. The cab stops by the kerb a few feet away from the entrance to the Serbian restaurant.

It's early—not even eleven o'clock—so I don't know if anyone will even be inside. I pay the driver and wait on the sidewalk until he drives away. This is a rundown area. With my niqab I stand out like a sore thumb and a few people stare at me.

I approach the door and expect it to be locked, but it opens when I push it, the bell tingling over my head. I pause, scanning the empty dining room, expecting someone to appear from the kitchen to see who just wandered in off the street. But no one does.

I go to the opposite end of the fragrant room, breathing in the scent of meats and veggies roasting in the kitchen, and walk out to the garden. I stop in the doorway, so damn relieved I can't speak, I can't think, and my breath comes out in gasps.

Dragan is standing on the patio, his back to me, looking out over the garden.

As if he can feel my stare, he turns to find me frozen in the doorway. A confused expression crosses his features.

The niqab. He can't see my face. I hurriedly tear the veil away.

An expression of such tender love crosses his face it snatches the air from my lungs. The moment lasts only seconds. His light eyebrows meet and suddenly he looks furious. I've never seen him so angry.

"What are you doing here?" he snarls. He isn't forming his words with care now.

I can't move, can't answer.

He strides over to me and grabs my upper arms. "Why the hell are you not on the train?"

"I couldn't leave … not without you. There must be another way."

"You have endangered yourself and Janna." He squeezes my arms, but not painfully. For once, I can see exactly what he's feeling. He's angry, but also scared. "That was stupid."

"I know," I say, staring him boldly in the face, not bothering with excuses. Well, I'm here, and I've no intention of leaving. Now what should we do?

He folds me into his arms and leans to kiss me, his passion just as hot as his anger. I open my lips to him, and lose myself to the rising heat and the sensation of his tongue probing into my mouth. He pulls back to meet my eyes, the familiar electricity sizzling in the space between us.

"I am supposed to see the Don later today. To tell him the job is done and show him the proof. I have always completed a contract for which I have been paid."

My stomach drops, but I can't pull away from this man now, no matter what dark things lie in his past. We're bound together now. I love him, and I'll climb any mountain, cross any sea to keep him.

"Killing was nothing to me, but something changed when I saw you. I just could not take your life. And now," he pauses, his light eyes burning into mine. "Now I love you. I would rather take my chances with the Don and lose my life than cause you harm."

My heart leaps with joy. He loves me. My God! He loves me.

"Oh, darling. I love you so much I thought I was going to die without you," I gush happily.

"You're not going to die. They have to kill me first."

I look up at him unhappily. All the problems are still there.

"Where is Janna?"

"She is safe. I've sent her to stay with an old friend. No one would think to look for her there."

He looks around. "Cover your face. You cannot be seen. I must know you're safe before I can make my plans. Can you go and stay with this friend?"

I nod and fix the veil over my head.

"How did you get here?"

"Taxi."

"Come on," he says taking my hand. We get out of the restaurant. I can see his car parked across the road, but he doesn't walk towards it. Instead he whispers, "Wait here," and starts walking down the road. Suddenly he turns into the next alleyway. I don't understand what he is doing. I know he said wait there, but my feet follow him, moving quicker and quicker. I arrive at the narrow alleyway. There are bins there. To my horror I see Dragan drag a man behind the bins. I can't move. My mind goes blank. As I stand there frozen he re-appears. We stop and we stare at each other.

I open my mouth but no words come out. He sighs and walks toward me.

"He saw you with me," he says softly, as if that is all the explanation I would need.

"I've got my veil on," I croak.

"Don't underestimate your enemy, Raven. That is the best way to get us all killed."

"Who is he?"

"A mutual acquaintance. He was just there at the wrong time and place. I couldn't take the chance. I need the element of surprise."

My eyes widen. That man died because of me. I go numb. The reality of him killing so easily hits me like a ton of bricks. Hearing that he is a killer didn't really affect me at all. Seeing how he took that man out in seconds behind the bin and the practical unemotional way he talks about it makes my whole body go cold.

He walks towards me, his face is closed, a stranger. "It is not too late to change your mind. You can still use your passports and start a new life abroad."

I look into his eyes. "I love you. I don't know what made you the way you are, but you are not that. It's what you do not what you are."

He blinks and stares at me.

"You are good and kind and one day you will see what I see."

He slips his hand under my veil and touches my face. "We don't have much time."

"What are you going to do?" I ask, suddenly frightened by the determined set of his jaw and the fire glowing in his eyes. Something unlocked in him and I can suddenly see the man behind the façade and how angry he is.

"I have to kill the Don," he says calmly. "And his son. There is no other way."

He frowns when I gasp at the idea of him killing another two people. Considering they were quite happy to have me killed I shouldn't have too much difficulty wishing them harm, but the thought that he will have to do the job hurts me.

"Letting either of those men live will mean we will always be looking over our shoulder, and believe me you don't want that. Russians never forget. So it's them or us."

"Wait. You know, the friend that Janna is staying with, her man is Nikolai Smirnov."

His eyebrows rise. "Your friend is Smirnov's girlfriend?"

"Yes, and she said that he would help."

"Yes, Raven, he is a very powerful man, but he cannot help. Nobody wants to be dragged into this kind of trouble."

"Please let me call her. You never know."

"No, I don't trust them. They stick together. No one must know our plan."

"Please, you have to trust me. Just the same I knew where to find you I know that we must ask Nikolai for help."

He shakes his head.

"Please, Dragan. Please."

"You don't understand this business, Raven. There is no such thing as friends. Nikolai doesn't even know me, but he does know and has done business with Sergei in the past. No one wants to make a powerful enemy when they don't have to."

"I don't know about any of that. I just know what I know." I press my hand to my solar plexus. "Here. It leads to you and I know it is the right thing to do."

He exhales. "This is a mistake, Raven."

"No, it's not."

"Why should Nikolai help me?"

"Because Star owes me."

"And you trust him to deliver on her behalf?"

"Would you do it for me?"

"Yes."

I smile. "Then I trust him."

He sighs.

"I don't know much about the word of the Mafia don, but I imagine they live in heavily guarded homes. How likely is it that you can go into the Don's lair, past all his men, and kill both him and his son without any help at all?"

"I know the layout of his house so I have a pretty good chance."

"Pretty good is not good enough for me."

"I'm afraid that's the best anyone can expect in this situation."

"Please, just go with my gut feeling. Just this once."

He frowns, but he nods. "Come on, let's get to the car before anyone else sees us," he says.

We walk briskly. Even more people stare at us now, because we make such an odd couple. A blond god and a woman with only her eyes visible. He takes off like a bat out of hell before I even have my seatbelt on. While I am in the car, I use his phone and call Star.

CHAPTER THIRTY-SEVEN

DRAGAN

*R*aven's friend turns out to be a flawless beauty who could not do enough for us. She meets us at the front door and takes us into the library of their home to meet her man. He stands from his desk and walks up to us. He is an inch taller than me and impeccably dressed in a suit. He looks as if he has been pulled out of a business meeting. He smiles but his eyes are cold and indifferent. Star makes the introductions.

"Dragan," he murmurs.

He takes my hand in a firm grip. "I've heard of you."

My eyebrows rise. I'm not sure I like this man.

"It's a compliment. From a satisfied customer," he says smoothly.

I hear Raven draw her breath sharply. She has stepped into the brutal world where people are complimented for killing other people.

Nikolai Smirnoff turns towards Star and smiles at her. A sense of relief rushes through my veins. Raven is right. He will do it for his woman. She goes over to him, gives his cheek a chaste kiss, and whispers something in his ear. His hand comes around her waist and he nods and strokes her hair gently. A secret look passes between them. Tearing her eyes away she turns toward Raven. "Come on. Let's get you something to eat."

Raven glances at me and my heart feels as if it is breaking. She is so pale and her eyes huge with fear. Her chin trembles. I want to hold her and tell her everything's going to be all right, but I can't. Not yet. I just smile at her and a ghost of one flickers on her lips.

"Come on," Star urges.

"I love you," Raven mouths to me and follows her.

The door shuts behind them.

"Drink?"

I refuse. I need a completely clear head.

We sit opposite each other. "What can I do for you?"

"There are many places a man like me could go and be forgotten, but not with a woman and child."

He nods slowly. This man says less than me.

I outline my plan, and he listens without interrupting. When I finish, he nods again.

"I can improve on your plan," he says, and smiles. A cold smile that does not reach his eyes.

Raven

*J*anna is asleep and Dragan and I are in one of the many bedrooms in Nikolai's grand house. Dragan presses me into his body and kisses me, our mouths desperate for the taste of each other.

It could be the last time we kiss.

"Tell me I'll see you again," I whisper, my lips moving over his. I'm so close I can see all the golden flecks in his eyes.

"I want to see you again more than I want anything else in the world," he says.

It's not the answer I want to hear. "I pray to God to bring you back to me."

"If I don't come back—"

I thrust my hand between us and lay my palm across his mouth. "Don't."

He kisses my palm.

"I wish we could just run away. I'm so afraid for you, Dragan."

"*We* can't run away, but promise me you'll leave for Paris and follow the plan if you don't hear from me before the end of tonight."

I nod, my stomach clenching at the thought of leaving the city without knowing if he's alive or dead. "I promise."

"If I don't make it I want you to know, I'm sorry I was so rough with you at the castle. It is my greatest regret. I think I was trying to push you away, treat you like a whore. Pretend you were just another woman I picked up, but nothing worked. You wriggled your way into my heart."

"You make me sound like a worm," I say in a watery voice.

"God, I wish I could make love to you now," he groans.

"Me too."

"If I make it back I'm going to fuck you so hard and long you're not going to be able to walk properly for days."

"You better make sure you come back. I hate men who make empty promises."

He chuckles. "Do you know what I thought when I saw you at the casino for the first time?"

"No. What?"

"I thought: fuck, man. You're in so much trouble. You were the hottest fucking thing I'd seen in all my life."

I grin. "Do you want to know what I thought?"

He flashes a panty-dropping smile and my stomach flips. "Sure."

"Well, I thought: Shit, Raven. Don't even look in that direction. He is waaaaaaay out of your league."

"I've never felt like this ever. I don't want to be separated from you."

He lowers his mouth to my ear. "When you told me you had seen Sergei's son's face it felt like a knife in my chest. No matter what happens, I'll never regret you."

A scream builds somewhere inside me. This is so unfair. I can't give up this man. I don't want him to go. I don't care if we spend the rest of our lives in a tiny remote village in Argentina. "I don't want you to go," I sob.

"Shhh ... I have to do this for us. For Janna. For our children when they come."

I start crying softly. "I'm sorry," I sniff. "I want to be strong for you, but I am so afraid."

"Don't be afraid. I have been through worse."

I look up at him hopefully. "Really?"

He nods.

"You will be careful, won't you?

"Do you think I want to lose you? Lose our life together? Remember when I told you I was the best. I wasn't exaggerating. If anybody can do this, it's me."

I nod, but my guts are twisted up with anxiety and fear.

"There you go. Now, I should leave."

We kiss again, deeply, my finger twining in his hair and praying this isn't the last time I'll see him.

CHAPTER THIRTY-EIGHT

DRAGAN

https://www.youtube.com/watch?v=7HKoqNJtMTQ
(This is the end...)

When Sergei is in England he lives in a secure complex outside the city. He is there today; waiting for me. Normally, this trip is never necessary. He reads about my work in the newspapers while enjoying his breakfast, or a courier brings him the photographs, or when I was younger and more gregarious, a little memento.

Still, he agreed to see me willingly enough. Sergei enjoys a whiskey with me. He once told me that I reminded him of himself when he was young.

It takes forty minutes to reach the complex with its high walls and gated entrance. I carefully go through my plan again as I turn off the A316 and get into Richmond. Getting in will not be a problem. Getting out alive would have been almost impossible, but with Nikolai's help there is a good chance I'll make it.

The armed guards at the gate wave me in without trouble. I was here two days ago. I continue down the long driveway to the main house, taking note of the guard dogs roaming the property. I know Sergei has at least four, but it is daytime and there are only two on patrol. They are obviously excellent at what they have been trained to do, though. I feel a little regret that such beautiful creatures must be sacrificed, but I have no choice.

I park my car and walk up to the house. A gardener is meticulously pruning a topiary in the shape of a deer. He does not even glance at me. He has a long way to go before he finishes his job. Good. He will be my witness later. Two men come out of the house and walk off to the side. They are kitchen staff. They notice me but do not smile or acknowledge me. No one stops me.

Fifty meters to my left there is a security house with armed guards. They stand very still and stare at me. There will be at least another two of them inside the house.

I knock on the LA style tall doors, and enter when a large, beefy man in a badly-fitting black suit opens it. Another two equally intimidating men stand with their feet apart and watch with dour expressions. I raise my arms to either side of me, and the man who opened the door frisks me thoroughly for weapons. His hands move briskly and professionally all over my body. He finds nothing and steps back.

"Where is Sergei?" I ask.

"In his office." His accent is thick and there is not an ounce of friendliness in his face.

"And Viktor?" Viktor is Sergei's son, the one Raven saw in the alley. He killed a man at the back of the casino over a petty dispute, risking everything because he cannot control his temper.

"He is there too. Come with me."

I nod and follow him past two more cold-eyed Russian goons. If I am fortunate everything will go to plan. My mission is simple. I need to kill Sergei. Viktor is incompetent and disliked by others in the organization. Once his father is dead, the power vacuum will ensure someone will end his life shortly thereafter.

The door to the office is closed. His security man knocks once.

Sergei calls something in Russian.

The door opens and I walk in.

"It's the help," Viktor sneers sarcastically. His father pays me, and that makes me a servant in his eyes, but it is more than that. He is jealous of me.

His father glances at him, but says nothing.

I step past the threshold, and the big man closes the door behind me. The three of us are alone in the room. Sergei is seated behind his desk.

"The job is done?" he asks.

I nod.

"Prove it," Viktor says.

Ignoring him, I keep my eyes on Sergei. Most likely both are armed, but if I can take out the father, the true threat in this room, Viktor, the shitbag will be too stunned to react.

My heart rate increases slightly, the way it always does before a kill, but my fingers are steady and my breathing calm. There is even a smile on my face. Outward nervousness makes men like this suspicious.

I pull a cellphone from my pocket.

"Yes, I have a photo."

Viktor walks around the desk to stand beside his father. I bring up the photo of Raven I took that night. Her chest covered in pig's blood as she lies on the ground pretending to be dead. I place my phone on the desk a little further away from Sergei than would make it comfortable for him to simply look down and see the photo. In the time it takes them to lean over to see the image, I whip up the small knife hidden inside the heel of my shoe.

The movement causes Sergei to look up. He does not have time to react. His mouth opens. "I—" he begins, but gets no further.

I hurl the knife at him. Years of training delivered in a split-second. Bullseye. The knife stabs his throat just under the Adam's apple. There is no way to bring a man back from such a wound. His eyes bulge as his hands come up to grab his throat. A futile gesture. Blood pours down his hands. He'll be dead in a minute. While I sat going through my plan minute by minute, going through every unexpected scenario that could possibly arise, I never envisioned this being so easy.

"What the hell have you done?" Viktor screams as he reaches for his own weapon. I launch myself at the arrogant bastard and as my body slams into his, his gun discharges. The sound is amplified by the room's hard floors and high ceilings. Good. The security guards will be here in seconds. If they didn't hear Viktor's cowardly shouts, they definitely would have heard the gunshot.

We land on the ground. While he is lying there winded, I smash his jaw with a power punch calculated to knock out a man twice his size. I don't want to kill him. He's out cold instantly. I glance around. Sergei falls sideways next to his son, gasping and reaching for me. I step back out of his grasp.

This is all his doing.

I hear heavy footsteps in the hallway, more than one set, charging down towards me. I lock the door—a momentary obstacle at best. I pick up Viktor's gun from the floor and reach into Sergei's jacket for his. He has stopped moving and his eyes are wide open. Outside, the men start ramming and kicking the door. They are thickset gorillas and they will burst through any moment.

I lie back on the table with both my hands up and ready. If I must die today, I am ready. I will die a happy man if I can secure Raven's and Janna's future.

As the door flies open I spray them with slugs. They unleash a hail of bullets that smash the table I am on. A bullet buzzes past close to my head. A stab of pain punches into my thigh as I continue to shoot. The chambers in my gun are not yet empty and three men are sprawled on the ground, their hulking bodies riddled with lead. I assess my wound quickly. It hurts like a bitch, but it's just a flesh wound. Enough to slow me down, but not stop me. I have dealt with far worse.

I take two guns from the dead men and hurry to the window. Opening it, I climb through and drop onto the manicured lawn. The guards communicate with one another via earpiece, so by now, they will all know the shots were fired in Sergei's office.

I set off at a lurching run to the front of the house. Someone calls out. Orders me to stop. I run harder. I keep running, not looking back, not taking the time to see how close they are to me or how many there are. I assume the worst and work from there, picking up speed to avoid being taken out right there on the grass. I need to make it back to where the gardener is.

Something catches on my foot and I go sprawling to the ground, landing hard, grunting at the agony that shoots up my leg. Before I can turn around properly a devil-faced snarling, foaming Rottweiler pounces and sinks its teeth into my calf. Oh Fuck.

No time to think.

I empty two taps into his head. His jaws loosen and the carcass falls away from me. The other dog is charging. I feel more regret to put a slug into it than I did those human beings I just killed. It falls with a whimper and stays still. I drag myself up, blood pouring from my wounds, and carry on running.

The guards are shouting at one another and getting closer.

I need to find cover quickly. To reach a hiding spot before I am eliminated out here in the open. I spot a rose arbor a few meters ahead. Shots whizz past me. Shit! They're gaining on me.

I drop to my hands and knees and half-crawl, half-roll towards the arbor. I pull myself upright and lean against the wooden structure. I picture Raven's face. I am ready to resign myself to dying in a hail of gunfire if I know I died for her. I saved her life. I did something good.

Sergei's remaining men are almost upon me. I know what I

have to do.

I struggle to my feet, swaying. There are six of them. They are spreading out so that I won't be able to protect myself from all sides. Too late for that, fuckers. They are not dealing with an amateur. I aim and start firing. I know which ones to take down first. They don't see me. After the first two go down the men start running for cover. There is none of course. Now they are the sitting ducks. I take them out. All six.

I don't have a lot of ammo left. My only hope of survival is to make it to the front of the house.

I drop to the ground and roll as fast as I can down the grassy slope. I still have some bullets and I *will* take out as many as I have to if they find me.

I may die, but Raven will be safe.

As the shouts of more men coming grow closer, I picture her and Janna on an island far away. Where the sea is blue and sun is hot. Raven will wear a red bikini and Janna will build sandcastles. I can join them if I can just make it to the front of the house.

I stand up and start running as fast as I can. I am so hyped up on adrenalin there is no longer any pain. As I reach the front I see the gardener cowering on the ground. He is my witness. He will see what happens next and tell Viktor. Beside my car I see two other cars parked there that were there before. I start running towards my car.

A door of one of the cars opens and Nikolai comes out. He takes out a gun and points it at me. There is no emotion on his face. I freeze. This is the moment I warned Raven about. The Russians always stick together. He will betray me. She said trust her. Trust her gut. He has the drop on me. The gardener watches. I raise my gun at him.

He pulls the trigger.

White-hot pain explodes in my chest. I drop to my knees and fall forward. It is Raven's face that I see before the darkness comes.

Always Raven. My Raven.

CHAPTER THIRTY-NINE

RAVEN

"Why can't we stay here forever and ever, Mummy," Janna asks.

"Because this is not our home." We are living in Nikolai's home in Surrey and Janna has been having a grand ole time, exploring the massive house and grounds, playing with their dog and being taken for rides on their horses.

"But I love it here," she moans.

"I know you do, but how would you like to live in a house by the sea? As soon as you step out of the front door you step on to the beach."

Her eyes widen. "Oh, Mummy, can we?"

"Yes, we'll go there in a week's time."

"Is that in two days?"

"Nope, that is in seven days. Count it on your fingers."

She starts counting using her chubby fingers and my heart

feels as if it will break with love for her. She shows me seven fingers.

"Well done, darling."

"Mummy, can we take one of the ponies from here? They have so many I don't think anybody will notice."

"Of course they will notice. When you take something without asking permission that is stealing."

"Shall I ask Star? I don't think she will mind."

"No, you cannot ask Star. Can we please stop talking about ponies?"

"All right."

"Raven," Betty, one of Star's staff calls.

I turn around.

"Do you mind if we take Janna to the village?"

I smile. "Of course." Everybody just loves Janna and she is becoming so spoilt here, but it makes me happy to see her showered with so much love and attention.

"Be a good girl," I say and kiss her.

"I will," she promises and skips away with Betty. As they leave the room I hear her say, "Can I have ice cream, Betty?"

"You can have anything you want," Betty says.

I stand up and open the door to the adjoining room. I tip-toe to the bed. Dragan is still asleep. His face looks pale. As I sit on the chair next to him, it creaks and his eyes are suddenly open and alert. "Hey, Beautiful," he mumbles.

"Sorry, I didn't mean to wake you up," I whisper.

"If I can wake up to the sight of you for the rest of my life, I will count myself the luckiest man alive."

"Let's see if you're still saying that in a year's time when you are no longer incapacitated," I tease.

"I'll show you incapacitated. Is that door locked?"

I giggle. "If you're so virile go check it yourself."

He makes to sit up and I stop giggling and lean forward, putting my hand on his arm worriedly. "Hey, don't do that. You'll tear your stitches."

He lies back down and shoots me a seductive grin. "How about a strip tease?"

"How about some stimulating conversation instead?" I counter.

"How long are you going to keep this up?"

"Until you get better," I say primly.

"Just flash me your boobs, then," he says with a naughty wink.

I look at him sternly. "Look you. I'm not taking any chances with you. The doctor told me about the risk of tearing your stitches."

"You're worried about my stitches tearing, I'm worried about my balls exploding. I'm so turned on by you all the time and I can't do a damn thing about it. You come in here in your sexy little cropped tops and your tight jeans and you lean over me and brush your body against mine and you expect me not to respond." He grasps my wrist in his hand. "Raven, I want you so bad I don't think I can carry on if I don't have you."

"Nice try. NO!"

"You're a hard woman, Raven Hill."

"Not as hard as that bullet they pulled out of your chest," I say referring to the bullet Nikolai shot into the area just above his heart. If I had known that was the plan I would have been terrified and never agreed to it. God, to think. If he had missed. At first, I was almost hysterical when they brought him back bleeding and almost dead. I didn't understand why Nikolai had to shoot him in the first place.

Then Star explained it to me.

The plan was for Viktor to think that Nikolai had helped him by shooting Dragan and killing him. Of course, since Nikolai's bullet was in Dragan's body, it was quite in order for him to insist that he would dispose of the body himself to ensure his bullet did not end up where it shouldn't. No one understands paranoia better than the Mafia.

Later that evening when I was talking to Dragan and I asked him about that moment when he had to stand there and allow Nikolai to shoot him, he admitted that for one second when Nikolai lifted the gun and aimed it at him, he didn't know if Nikolai would betray him in favor of his Russian friends, and not just shoot to wound but to kill. When he said that I shivered to think what he had been through for me, for us.

The plan now was that we would stay here until Dragan had healed a little, then we would quietly fly to a tiny island Dragan owns. We will stay there until Viktor is toppled from his perch. Once he is gone we will be safe to come back to England.

"Why not kill Viktor?" I asked, confused that they had let him live.

Star explained that Viktor is a fool compared to any of the men who would have stepped in to fill Sergei's shoes if Viktor too had been killed that day. Nikolai and Dragan knew it would be much harder to persuade them to believing the lie that the gardener and the other staff cowering in the house saw. That Nikolai had shot and killed Dragan.

I don't know what I would have done without Star. She made me feel petty for the way I held a grudge against her all those years. That time when I was sick with worry she couldn't do enough. She even sat up with me during the night. We talked a lot. We held each other and cried because we had been stupid enough to let a man get between us. I've always loved Star, even when we were not on speaking terms, I could never hate her or not wish her well. She is my sister, pure and simple, just like Cindy.

I look down at Dragan, my beautiful blond man, sleeping peacefully in the gloom, and love and gratitude flows through my body.

"It's dark in here. Will you open the curtains just a bit?" he asks.

"Of course." I go over to the window, draw the curtain halfway and come to stand by his bed.

"Will you reach for my water?" he asks.

I lean over him to get the glass. In a flash his hand comes out and grabs me. I squeal with surprise as I am lifted off my feet. The next I know I am lying on top of him. I look at him in horror. "My god, Dragan. Your stitches."

"Fuck the stitches, Raven. If they tear, just give me a needle and thread, and I'll sew them up myself."

"You're crazy."

"Yeah, that's right. I'm going ape shit crazy over your blue eyes and black hair here. Do a sick man a favor and toss him a quick kiss, will you?"

His breath is hot and delicious against my ear. He has no idea I'm dying to make love with him again. Lying on him like this is just pure temptation, but the last thing I want to do is hurt him. I'm not an animal, I can wait.

"Just one quick peck?" I ask.

"Of course. It's not like I can do much in my condition."

I dip my face and let my lips touch his. It is supposed to be a chaste kiss, but his hand tightens on my body and pulls me deeper into the bed. Now I am lying over his body.

"Your thigh," I warn.

"Forget about my thigh. Feel this," he says and grinds me against his cock. Thick, hot, and throbbing it digs into my flesh. Desire ricochets through my body, and fire runs through my veins. This thing with him … it's so hard to resist. I've never felt like this before. His palm is between my legs, the heat from it growing, maddening me.

I know I shouldn't.

I lift my head and stare at his lips. "You said one quick …" I begin.

"I talk too fucking much," he growls and claims my mouth again.

This time I don't protest.

EPILOGUE

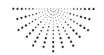

Raven
(Six months later)
At an undisclosed island in the Pacific Ocean

I wiggle my toes in the sand and lift my chin to enjoy the heat of the sun on my face. Before I met Dragan I'd only ever been to overcrowded beaches with my parents. Now I wake up to the sound of the waves crashing into the shore.

"Look at me!" Janna calls.

I open my eyes to see her running at the water's edge. She has a swimsuit for every day of the week. Today, she's wearing her polka dot bikini, but she has matched it with a blue and pink piece from one of her other suits. I don't believe I've ever seen her wear a matching two-piece before.

I'm wearing a bikini too, but for a different reason. My stomach has swollen to beyond what a one-piece can safely contain. The baby moves and kicks. I swear sometimes he's doing cartwheels in there. I rest my hands on my stomach and send my love to the life in there, growing. Any day now, I'll meet our baby. Janna's little brother.

I think of Octavia. How I would have loved to have shared this pregnancy with her. If she could only see Janna now. Maybe she is looking down on us. If she is, she will see how happy her daughter is.

I wave at Janna and she goes back to her game of running towards the water when it recedes and running away when it advances, laughing like mad the whole time. She's played the same game since we came. She never seems to grow tired of it.

"Are you okay?"

I look up to find Dragan standing above me, smiling warmly, offering the glass of pineapple juice I asked him to fetch from the house.

"I'm fine," I say, rubbing my tummy. "The baby's just doing gymnastics." I down the glass of juice in three gulps. I blame the baby. He's always thirsty nowadays.

Dragan drops down beside me. His chest isn't giving him much trouble anymore. The gunshot wound was never as serious as I imagined. Nikolai is a crack shot. We're new people living new lives in this tropical paradise.

Dragan lays his warm palm on my stomach and smiles when the baby moves beneath his hand. "He's a strong lad."

I laugh. "Like his Daddy."

He smiles again.

"Do you think Janna will be jealous?"

He shakes his head. "No."

"How can you be so sure?"

"Because she inherited her mummy's big heart."

He puts his arm around me and I lean my head onto his shoulder. "I've kind of decided on a name for him."

"Oh yeah?"

I raise my head and look into his beautiful eyes. "Yeah. I want to call him Luka. Unless you don't want to, of course,"

"My father's name," he says almost in wonder.

I nod.

"Thank you," he says, and there are tears in his eyes.

"Watch me!" Janna calls. She charges into the water now and belly flops onto a wave.

Both Dragan and I laugh at her antics.

"Are you happy?" Dragan asks after a few moments of watching Janna at play.

I answer without hesitation. "I'm so happy sometimes I can't believe it's not just a dream." We're safe and together, which is all that matters. I miss seeing Cindy every day, but we've been in contact. Dragan knows how to do this securely. One day, hopefully soon, I'll be able to see her again.

"Are you happy?" I ask him.

He kisses the top of my head. "Yes," he says. "I have what I always wanted. A family of my own."

He never talks about his family and I don't push him, but the promise of the baby has changed him in ways I wouldn't have believed possible. That old ice-cold man is gone forever. Replaced by the father of my unborn child and Janna. He promised me he will never go back to what he did before and he has kept his word. He says even to think of what he did sickens him now.

We're a family now. We're safe. We're together.

The rest of the world can wait.

Raven
(Two Months Later)
Still at an undisclosed island in the Pacific Ocean

https://www.youtube.com/watch?v=EXfLirBwBKY
(Time to tell her everything)

I run blindly away from our house.

I run because I am so hurt and angry. I run because after all these months Dragan has finally told me what happened to his mother. How he searched for the men for years and years, long after the hostilities had eased in the region and everybody had forgotten it. Finally, he tracked down the only man whose face he saw in a bar in Morocco. How he took him and tortured him until he revealed the identity of all the other men. How he found them one by one and killed them all.

My heart is broken for that innocent six-year old boy. What he had to go through. What he suffered all these years. I run to the little waterfall in the woods. I sit on a rock, hold my swollen belly, and burst into tears.

A branch cracks behind and I try to stop the tears. I don't want him to see me crying. I want to be strong for him. I blink back the tears. His strong arms come around my body and I start to sob. I feel angry with myself for being so weak. I should be comforting him. I dash the tears away and turn around.

"Oh, Dragan, I'm so, so sorry about what happened to your mother. I wish I could do something, but I can't," I sob.

"Shhh … you mustn't cry for her. She is in heaven with the angels. All around her are fruit orchards and fields of flowers."

I stare into his eyes. Once they were dead, now they are pools of color that reflect his beautiful soul.

I take a deep breath. "You'll see her again."

He smiles sadly. "No, I won't. I won't be going to the same place as her.

I've accepted that."

"You don't know that."

"I don't know that, but I hope it is that way. There should be a place specially for the good and the innocent. A place that cannot be tainted by people like me."

I take both hands and put them on either side of his face. "You are not a bad person. If you're not a good person, I don't know who is. I'm blessed because of you. I'm alive because of you. Whatever you did, you did because this cruel world turned the heart of a child of God to stone. I'm going wherever you are."

Raven
(Eighteen Months Later)
England

"Happy Birthday, darling," I say happily.

"Thanks, Mummy." She sounds shy. Every day I see her changing and I don't like it. A year ago she would have wrapped her arms around my head and said, "What present have you got for me?" Now she's behaving like an adult. Thanking me.

"What would you like to have for breakfast, hmmm?"

"Pancakes," she says.

"What a good idea"

"Is Luka awake yet?"

"Nah, that sleepyhead kept both of us awake all night and now he is fast asleep."

She giggles.

"Anyway, don't you want to know what present daddy and I have for you?"

She nods.

I hold my hand out. "Come on then."

She slips her hand into mine and I lead her to the kitchen. I open the kitchen door and we both stand on the tiled patio.

She looks around. "What is it?" she asks.

At that moment, Dragan appears from the side of the house. He is leading a pony.

I let go of her hand, take a step forward and watch her. Her mouth drops open and then she begins to cry. When I see her crying, I start crying too. Bawling her little heart out, she starts walking stiffly towards the pony. Still crying loudly, she wraps her little arms around the pony's neck and lays her cheek on it.

"Do you like him?" Dragan asks.

The poor mite nods and continues sobbing.

Dragan comes to me. "Hey," he says. "Why are you crying?"

"I don't know," I howl.

From somewhere upstairs comes a yell.

"That's all I need," Dragan says, and runs upstairs to get Luka.

I walk towards Janna and crouch next to her. "Are you happy?"

"Yes," she says, and launches herself into my arms as she has done since she was a baby. We are both still crying when Dragan comes with Luka. He is yelling his head off too. Dragan stands there at a loss.

Suddenly both Janna and I start laughing. Tiny Luka stops howling and stares at the new pony. This is my family. This is my life.

I love it.

The End

COMING SOON...

THE HEIR

I thought he was a player.
How could I have possibly known what he really was?

Georgia Le Carre

CHAPTER 1

ROSA

"*C*iao Bella."

The voice is dripping honey with a hint of something dark and delicious. But that trite phrase. Someone please stop me from picking up my fork and stabbing it into his crotch. I let my eyes wander upwards. Hang on! That is one full crotch. Looks like there is something very large tucked away beneath those fine black trousers. Hmmm...

A little higher. All right. The man works out. If my washing machine packs up I could wash my clothes on his abs.

I let my eyes travel even higher. Did someone say pecs and abs? Drool, drool.

Whoa. Open shirt.

Two buttons undone: check.

Chest hair: check.

Gold chain: check.

St Tropez tan: check.

Black hair curling over the collar: Check.

What a shame. Mediterranean playboy, obviously. Still, I'm a sucker for a brown throat.

No, no, no, not a chin dimple as well. A little above the lickable dimple a sensual mouth is slightly twisted into a mocking smile. Yup, life's just not fair.

Eyes. Jesus. H. Christ. Pools of whiskey that you just want to drown in. There's no longer any doubt. He's obviously slept with tons of women.

The mouth opens. "You know, I've never banged a bridesmaid before."

Why does God make such good-looking assholes? "Looks like today's not your lucky day either," I say as dryly as I can.

The smug smile becomes wider, the man is oozing confidence and something else. Something that makes me want to bite him. He lowers that wonderful body into the chair opposite. "On the contrary, I think today is that day."

"Oh yeah? How do you reckon that? There are three of us. Raven is pregnant, Cindy is taken, and I'm not interested."

He leans back and looks at me curiously. "What makes you think you're not interested?"

"What makes you think I am?" I counter.

"Because I'd make the perfect one-night stand."

I look at the rose petal floating in my glass of champagne. Star will be so irritated to see it. She expressly said she didn't want it. I look into his mesmerizing eyes. "I'm not looking for a one-night stand."

He grins. He has splendid teeth. All white and gleaming. "Ah, but you are a career woman. You have no time for relationships and long-term commitment."

Something in my belly melts. "I'm not sleeping with you."

"Who said anything about sleeping?"

There is very little air in my lungs suddenly. "I'm not fucking you."

"Ten bucks says you do."

"What would I do with ten bucks in this country?" I ask scornfully.

"I'll take you to America and you can spend it there."

"That's not how one night stands work."

"No, I meant I'll fly you there tonight. We'll have sex in a great hotel, then you can spend your money in the morning."

"If I have sex with you then I won't have the ten bucks to spend, will I?"

"You'll have more than ten bucks." He takes an expensive looking wallet out of his trouser pocket and fishes out five crisp hundred-dollar bills and lays them on the table."

WTF! My eyes widen with shock. I look at the money and his large, bronzed hand, a gold watch peeping from a snowy white sleeve, slowly sliding away on the white tablecloth. How dare he? Calmly, I take my gaze back to his face. "First of all five hundred dollars? How cheap are you? And second do I look like a prostitute to you?"

"First of all: Baby, come with me and I'll make this ten, twenty, fifty, or even a hundred thousand? Name your price." He shrugs. "Secondly: you don't pay a woman to have sex

GEORGIA LE CARRE

with her, you pay her to leave after sex, and we both know you'll probably sneak out in the morning before I wake up."

I cross my hands and his eyes drop to my breasts. "Excuse me. My face is up here buster."

"I know exactly where your face is, Bella. I was looking at your boobs."

I glare at him. "It's a bit sad when you have to flash Daddy's money around just to get laid."

"Very sad," he agrees with a grin, completely unaffected by my insult.

"Who are you?" I demand. He's obviously from the groom's side.

"I'm Dante D'Angelo, and you are Rosa."

My lips part. In spite of myself I'm flattered that he was interested enough to find out my name. "How do you know that?"

"I asked the bride."

I nod. "So how do you know the groom?"

"We're friends." For the first time, something in his eyes change. My mind notes the shift. He's not *all* player, there's something more beneath the glittering facade.

He leans forward slightly, his whiskey eyes swirling with desire. "Do you want to know what the bride told me?"

I frown. What on earth could Star have told him about me. "What?"

"She said, you would be perfect for me."

My eyes dart to the dancefloor. She is slow-dancing, her

cheek laying on her husband's chest. I don't know what I expected, but never that. She's usually so rational and down to earth. The stress of the wedding must have affected her so much she's told a pampered, Italian playboy I'm perfect for him. Either that or he's lying.

"Well, I'm not going to bed with you." My voice is absolutely firm. I'll never go to bed with a shallow beast like him. Never. Not in a million years. He can take his gorgeous teeth, and his splendid shoulders, and his laughing, teasing eyes, and his…his...full crotch, and shove it all up his ass.

CHAPTER 2

Rosa
Six weeks later

"You're what?" Star screams in my ear.

I hold the phone away. "I'm pregnant," I repeat.

"How?"

"The usual way, I guess?"

"Who?" Poor thing is so shocked she's shooting one word questions at me.

"You'll never believe me if I told you."

"Who?" she demands aggressively.

"Dante D'Angelo."

"What?" she explodes.

"Do you want me to repeat his name or are you just saying that for effect?"

"But you used a condom."

"Yeah, we did. I was thinking of suing the makers when I happened to read the packaging. Did you know that there is a one percent chance of getting pregnant even when you use a condom? It says so right here on the packaging."

"No."

"Those are terrible odds. God, if I had known earlier I would have made him wear two layers, but that would only reduce the odds to one in two hundred. We need a new invention. Either that or we'll all have to stop having all this sex and-"

"Rosa, are you okay?"

"What do you think? I'm calling you from my bathroom floor."

"Did you fall? Are you all right? Do you want me to come around?"

"No. Yes. No. I…err…am sitting propped up against the bath. I don't think it has properly registered yet. I'm saving my total meltdown for later."

She takes a deep breath. "Do you need an audience for that? I'm in Mayfair so I can pop around."

"It won't be pretty," I warn. I can already feel my body starting to shake. Mother of God, I'm pregnant.

"How many times did you do the test?"

"Five."

"Right. You're pregnant."

"You're hurting my ear, Star."

"Sorry."

"It's not your fault. It's that smooth talking bastard's fault. He got me into this. I've been having sex since I was seventeen, and nothing like this has ever happened. One night with that, that, pampered Casanova and I'm pregnant. Of all the damn men I could have got up the duff with I had to go do it with that shallow womanizer."

"Are you going to keep it?" Her voice is neutral, but I can hear the anxiety in it. Star loves kids. She coos at babies in the street and she's been buying and hoarding baby clothes for years now.

I have a sudden image of Dante's gleaming, taut body rippling as he thrusts into me. I hate him, obviously, but for god's sake, he removed my panties with his yummy teeth. And he was really, really, reeeeeally good at what he did. I couldn't walk properly for days afterwards.

"I don't know yet," I say, but even as I am saying it I have an image of a barefoot little boy with black hair and whiskey eyes running wild in a field, which is stupid because I live in one of the most concrete parts of London, and I'll have to drive at least an hour to find a field. And if I did I would never trust my child to run barefoot, because of rusty nails, dog poop, and whatever else is in open fields.

"Bastard," I curse soundly, as if it's all Dante's fault and I didn't beg for him to do it harder and faster.

"You mean you might keep it?"

"Maybe," I say slowly.

"Oh, Rosa. You should. It'll be such fun. I could take care of it while you are at work or when you go out at night. If it gets too much or you need a break you could drop it off at our place and-"

"Star," I interrupt. "do you mind. You're making it sound like the baby is a suitcase."

"Well, in a way it is."

"They scream all night."

"No, they don't."

"Yes, they do. I have first-hand experience. The brat next door never stops screaming all night."

"He has colic."

"What if my baby has it?" Jesus, I can't believe I said that. I'm thinking of the baby as a little person. My little person. All for me. "Oh, my God, Star. I think I'm going to keep the baby."

"You'll have to tell the father then," she gushes excitedly.

I thought I'd never see him again when I slipped out of his hotel room that morning while he was still asleep. Maybe, I haven't thought this decision out properly. I'm never not in a million years seeing that guy again.

Never.

And I mean never.

To be continued...

The Heir will be out in August. Until then hug a dog, eat some chocolate, kiss a good looking stranger and read some great books!

Or

Want to know more about Nikolai and Star?
Check out their story here.

UK --Submitting To The Billionaire
US --Submitting To The Billionaire
Australia --- Submitting To The Billionaire
Canada --- Submitting To The Billionaire

Thank you for reading Redemption!
To receive news of my latest releases and giveaways please click on this link.
http://bit.ly/10e9WdE
and remember
I **LOVE** hearing from readers so by all means come and say hello!
FACEBOOK

Printed in Great Britain
by Amazon

26017640R00169